# SHELTER

## TERRY HAYMAN

**SHELTER**

**Terri Hayman**

THE INTERVIEW SUBJECT, Professor Scott Stoker, lay in a wheeled hospital bed in a small, featureless room. He was covered by a sheet from the neck down. His face was battered and burned. But his blue eyes were sharp as he smiled at the young woman and the small digital recorder on the table beside her, its red recording light on.

"Did you ever see the experiment," he said, "near the end of World War Two, where Nazi scientists put a female rat in a maze that had no exit?"

Stoker paused and the young woman shifted awkwardly in her folding metal seat. Quite against her will she pictured a balding scientist in a white lab coat with thick glasses and a cruel mouth. The man dropped a small white rat into a table maze constructed of wood, with movable panels. The rat landed and the young woman could almost hear the skittering feet and racing heartbeat.

"The female rat had been trained to believe that there was a way out," Stoker continued, "and that it had to find it quickly or it would suffer painful electric shocks. When it couldn't find the exit, it panicked. Life or death."

The interviewer felt herself breathing faster now, seeing in her mind the rat running back into a corridor it has seen before. The little pink nose twitches erratically. The little heart is pounding.

"But here's the stroke of genius. They then put a male rat in with it. What do you think happened?"

The interviewer held her breath as she mentally saw the cruel-mouthed scientist drop in the second, larger rat.

"Not even going to try?" Stoker said. "Of course not. It's above your pay grade. You just want to know about Jasmine Kazmi. Who she was. What happened to her."

"I..." the interviewer began. "Of course. Tell me about Ms. Kazmi."

Stoker grimaced. "Ms. Kazmi. She was in my Advanced International Conflicts class. Had been all term, I assume. She'd also apparently been living with my son for a couple months. Had even come to our house. But honestly, the first time I became *aware* of her would have been, what? Two weeks ago? April 30th."

The interviewer gasped, then tried to hide it. It felt like Stoker had just punched her in the gut.

"Yes, you remember April 30, don't you? Spring weather. Every college student just wanted to get outside. Maybe study for final exams..."

THE BREEZE SEEMED to be urging the birds to sing as it rustled through the cherry blossoms ringing the quad. Soft green grass was couch and bed to scores of students. They called to others who walked the brick paths between the Victorian, brown brick buildings.

Inside one of those staunchly conservative buildings, the imposing Gowen Hall—it had once been the domain of the Faculty of Law, but was now the bearer of University of Washington's political science program—the second-last class of Advanced International Conflicts was in full swing. Professor Stoker strode back and forth down front like a handsome, aging lion. He was tall, square-chinned and blue-eyed, with a full head of silver hair that came almost down to the collar of his crisp white shirt. The wildness was echoed in the bright pink tie, but held in check by the dark-blue suit. Almost all the students filling the crowded stadium seating of his classroom were scribbling or leaning forward intently to catch his words, anything that might be on the upcoming final.

The one student who was not, was Jasmine Kazmi, "Jazz" to the few people who knew her well.

Seated midway back in the seats, she barely heard Stoker or the shuffling feet, creaking desks, smacking gum, air vents still pumping in heat despite the warm weather outside. Her entire focus was the sound of her own thumping heart and the buzz of thoughts spinning around and around like mad little mice in a panic. God, she needed a hit of something. Xanax, Valium, Atrivan, anything. She was perpetually wired these days. Constant state of panic. She couldn't settle. She couldn't...

The silent buzz of her phone in her lap made her almost jump from her chair. She grabbed the phone, lifted it, and discretely looked at the text. It was from Randy.

Meet you in Grieg Gardens. 3 pm. I'LL GET YOU FREE, JAZZ.

Her hand shook so hard she almost dropped the phone. And as she fumbled for it, afraid that others would notice, the sounds of the class came roaring in.

"...the South China Sea Talks!" Stoker thundered at the class. "*Major* escalation of tensions this week. The negotiating parties are messing up. Why? Be specific."

Hands shot up all over. It was that kind of group. Upper year. Smart. Very multi-ethnic. (Jazz was one of three Persians, there was a guy from Senegal, a bunch of Asians.) And everyone seemed totally into pleasing Stoker because his reputation went way beyond UW. He did an annual lecture circuit where he talked at other universities around the US and occasionally overseas. Rumor was he was going to be a speaker at a TED Talk this year. The big deal was that he usually selected a prize student from one of his classes to accompany him on tour as an assistant. If he was pleased with them, he might even agree to be their thesis advisor for post-grad studies. All of which practically guaranteed either a political internship or an associate professor's position somewhere.

Even Jazz had entertained that dream at the beginning of term. Back when it still seemed possible. When she'd been only half-broken from losing her dad. When her mom was still around to tell her she was brilliant and could do anything. Before that had all gone and she'd made so many stupid choices that now...

Well, now, her life was basically a daily sequence of terror and dog shit.

Stoker pointed to one of the students who had his hand up. He probably didn't know the kid's name. Probably didn't care. But the kid, slick and blond and fit looking, jumped up and plunged in like he'd been singled out as God's chosen.

"It's all about the economy," the kid said. "China's economy is crashing. People rioting. So they're trying to shift the focus by externalizing the enemy."

Stoker nodded. "'Externalizing the enemy.' Okay. How does that play out in the talks?"

The blond kid was about to answer but another dozen hands had shot up and Stoker pointed to one of them. Female. Chinese looking. That was probably deliberate on Stoker's part. Though when she stood and opened her mouth, the accent said born and raised in the USA, probably in LA.

"There's a low threshold of suspicion, especially post

COVID-19. China says they're historically entitled to the entire region. None of the parties trust each other. Nobody wants to make any concessions."

She started to sit down but Stoker gestured to her to stay as she was. "So a pressured, belligerent China," he summarized, "a shaken USA and other Asian countries. But what else did Frank say about powerful leaders? Practicality. Optimism."

The standing girl grinned. "The Chinese are optimistic they can walk all over us."

The class rippled with laughter.

A third student, short and intense, Jewish looking, jumped up without being called. That was a risky move in Stoker's class unless you had something really smart to say.

"The Japanese are keeping quiet," he said, "letting us do the negotiating. That's practical."

Stoker pinned him with his gaze and lowered his voice into a menacing purr. "Is that helping or hurting?"

That purr, like his son's, so unnerved Jazz that she dropped her pen. It skittered half under the desk beside her but when she ducked to pick it up she could just reach it. She came up to see Stoker directing his fearsome focus on her now.

"Ms. Kazmi. A comment?"

He knew her *name?* Shit. All evidence to the contrary. "I...um...what?"

"Should weaker parties sit back and let others speak for them?"

He gave her a tight smile and the entire class erupted at his cleverness. Jazz's face burned. She pursed her lips and looked down.

"And that," Stoker said, "is how sovereign states lose their place at the table."

That made Jazz lift her face just enough to see Stoker had turned back to the short, intense Jewish student he'd been about to eviscerate before Jazz dropped her pen. The kid had sat down again, probably realizing he'd dodged a bullet. But now Stoker was looking at him like he'd just thrown up all over himself. "How about you, Mr. Berman?"

"Pardon me?"

"You told us the Japanese had tricked us into doing the negotiating. I may be speaking to one of our negotiators. Should I tell him he's been duped?"

"Um..."

"Not an acceptable stall in high stake negotiations, Mr. Berman."

"I don't..."

"Tell me you don't know and don't bother showing up for the exam."

"But..." The kid was sweating. Coming apart.

"You want to fail this class?"

"I don't. I don't. I just don't...um..."

Jazz found herself on her feet. *Damn it. Damn it. Should have just let it go. Why couldn't I let it go?*

Stoker turned to her. "Ms. Kazmi?"

"China's going to start a war," she blurted. "The IJIC shows them funneling fissile material to North Korea and brokering an alliance with Russian."

Stoker stopped another kid who looked ready to respond. "You think Ma Yang could push the Politburo Standing Committee to cozy up to the Russian president? Really?"

"Sure," Jazz said. "Long enough to neutralize him while China prepares to take out the US." She blushed again. "I mean...I don't know. But it's classic Sun Tzu, right? All warfare's based on deception."

She sat down, dropping her gaze to avoid everyone's stare, and was saved by the clock ticking over. 2:50 p.m.

Stoker made a large, underhand wave. "Time. For the last class bring any questions you want to clear up. I'll go over the format of the final exam."

In the scramble of students packing up, Jazz grabbed the leather carry bag that doubled as her purse, stuffed her notes, text, and phone into it, and slung it over her shoulder. Then she tried to negotiate her way down the steps towards the exit as quickly as she could without touching anyone else.

"Ms. Kazmi," Stoker called to her and motioned her over.

No. No no no. She had to go *now*. Had to get to the Grieg Garden by three to meet Randy would be there. He might be her last hope.

Stoker motioned again and she reluctantly stepped closer. He smiled.

"Jasmine—Can I call you that?—that was very brave, standing up for another student like that. And you're usually such a meek little thing. I thought that was what my son liked about you."

Jazz shuddered. She saw other people notice, but couldn't help it.

Stoker saw it too. "Are you okay?"

Fine. Since she had to be talking to him, maybe... "Um, can I...ask you something, Professor?"

"Certainly. What is it?"

*Your son. He's a manipulative, cruel monster.* "Just that..."

But she couldn't. Didn't he know? If he did, he clearly didn't care. If he didn't know, he wouldn't believe her. And who would? She hadn't been able to believe it when he revealed himself.

"Nothing," she said. "Sorry. I'll...*we* will see you tonight."

"Right!" Stoker said. "Yes. It's been a while since Aaron's brought you over."

Her mouth tasting like she'd just swallowed acid, Jazz nodded and ducked out the door.

She headed for the south entrance of the building, assuming she'd avoid most of her classmates heading for the quad, but just as she cleared the rear and started toward the Grieg Garden, she heard, "Jazz. Jazz! Hey, Jasmine! Hey!"

Carly, Ava, and Beth, three perfectly nice girls she'd been friends with once upon a time when she still had a future. They were standing with the Berman kid, gesturing to her. Jazz ducked her head like she hadn't heard them and walked faster. Thankfully, they didn't follow.

Then she was into the garden. It was a paved, winding path, with rhododendrons and lavender around the bust of Edvard Grieg and grass, blue spruce, and bushes everywhere else. Jazz slowed her pace and looked for Randy. He was a big guy, bear sized, with a red beard and hair. Big enough, Jazz had been sure, to scare off Aaron. Why Randy had flirted with her, pursued her as he did when she'd basically come across as a door mouse, she didn't know. Except that maybe he'd seen her fear and need. Maybe he had this compulsion to rescue people. She remembered from one of the few psych electives she'd taken that certain people were rescuers.

But her bear-like redhead was nowhere to be seen. And everywhere she looked, every guy she saw lounging on the grass or walking slowly on the path looked a bit like Aaron to her – a nondescript, blandly handsome, almost skinny but wickedly brutal.

Heart hammering, Jazz ducked off the path and behind a tree. She pulled out her cell phone and checked for a text. Nothing. It was 3:05.

She typed in "I'm here. Where are u?" and sent it.

No response.

Oh God oh God.

She pulled up her stored phone contacts and scrolled to Women's Crisis Line. Hovered her finger over the number. It was time. She couldn't go on like this. If Randy wasn't going to save her, then—

She shrieked as a hand grabbed her by the shoulder and spun her around.

Aaron Stoker.

CHAPTER 3

"Aaron...," she blurted.

Aaron was three years older than her. Still in university as a grad student, going for his master's in political science to follow his father's path. He also had the smooth arrogance and square chin of her father, and maybe that's what had triggered some atavistic submission reflex in her when he'd first approached her, wooed her, offered to be her savior. But his grey, squinty eyes now were so wolf-like and cruel, Jazz wondered if they'd ever been different or she'd just been so needy she'd been willfully blind.

"Shh!" He put his finger to her lips. "I said meet me in the Wolf Den. What're you doing here?"

"I was hot," she said. Truth. "Not feeling well."

"You on something?"

"No, I..."

"Gimme your bag."

And without waiting, he ripped it from her shoulder and began rifling through it. He pulled out a bottle of Aspirin, her course book, notes, hairspray, gum, pens. He turned it over and dumped everything onto the grass. Felt the bag's lining like she might have a secret compartment.

Jazz wailed, "What are you doing? You bastard! I said I—"

He slammed her up against the tree so she dropped her phone. He saw it and crunched it with his foot.

"What do you need that piece of shit for anyway, right?" he said. "Can't call your mom anymore. Obviously don't feel the need to call *me* or answer my texts! That's gratitude."

He grabbed her throat, but, from the corner of his eye obviously saw someone watching and changed the choke to a deep kiss. Which was almost as suffocating, Jazz thought in panic, breathing hard through her nose. But at least he was playing the part fully now. Drawing back enough to let her breathe, stroking her cheek tenderly.

"Aw, honey. Look, I'm sorry. I'm sorry. I shouldn't be like that. That was stupid. That was unforgiveable but I hope you'll forgive me. I'll buy you another phone. Promise."

Almost like he meant it. After all, who could hear him now? And it was this shit, this being so apologetic, contrite, wanting to make things right, promising to never hit her again, never emotionally attack her again, that made the alternative of fighting back or reporting him to the police or...or...calling the Women's Distress Line...so damn hard. Like it was her fault somehow when he lost it.

"It's just," he went on, "I get so jealous when I find you've been seeing some other guy behind my back. Like you only let me take care of you because of my dad. Like who he is on campus made me respectable. Or safe somehow."

"I didn't even know that—"

"And now this other guy," he said. His hand had stopped just under her jaw, like he was ready to choke her again.

Jazz held very still as she said, "I'm not seeing anyone else."

His finger ran down her throat. "Okay. Okay. Good. Cause I talked to this guy called Randy just, like ten minutes ago, who seemed to think you'd promised him something. I convinced him to leave you alone."

He waited. Jazz said nothing. He leaned in close to her ear. From a distance it probably looked so loving.

"The dinner at my folks tonight? Eight p.m. I want you home by four to clean the apartment before you get ready, okay?"

"Okay," Jazz said.

"Good. Cause if you try to run away again, it's going to get ugly."

He straightened, turned, and strode off.

Jazz dropped to her knees and gathered up her personals from the grass. She brushed off the Stoker text, *International Treaties and Conflict Resolution*, and put it and everything else back into her bag.

Finally she picked up her phone. The front was cracked in an awful looking spider web, but it was still on. She pressed the still-open Women's Crisis Line and felt tears forming in her eyes as it actually dialed and rang. On the fifth ring, it was answered with a recorded message: "We're sorry. Everyone's away from the phone right now or dealing with other callers. Please leave your name and number and we'll call you back as soon as possible."

After the beep, Jazz said, "My name's Jasmine Kazmi."

She gave her number. "I live with Aaron Stoker in the Mallory Apartments. If you can't reach me when you call back, I may be dead."

CHAPTER 4

THE MALLORY APARTMENTS were just off campus on NE 47th Street. Clean, but not big or modern. The bathroom in the little bachelor Jazz shared with Aaron was frankly not even that clean. The tiles where cracked and there were marks in the tub that she hadn't been able to scrub out.

But the bathroom did have a lock on the door. It had become her favorite place in the apartment because of that.

It was where she sat now on the toilet at 5:45, holding a pregnancy test strip into her urine stream. When she was done, she placed the test strip carefully to one side, wiped herself, and stood up to straighten the party dress she'd put on for Aaron. It was tight. The mirror showed it was doing its job to emphasize her tits and ass the way Aaron liked. Totally inappropriate for a dinner with the parents, but maybe that was Aaron's point.

Maybe he even knew and relished how far the inappropriateness went.

Like the fact she hated the son of those parents. That she'd always been considered brilliant but Aaron had her so scared of him that she honestly believed she could never get away from him. He'd find her and beat her and beat her but never let her just die and be done with it. So it might be better if she just slit her wrists.

Except the tiny part inside her that was still fighting for survival stepped in when that distress got too great and did it's best to artificially help her through it. All the prescription anti-anxiety drugs. Or now, when she had to be *on*, a little baggie of cocaine she'd scored off a local street dealer on the way home. She pulled the baggie out of her bra, laid out a careful little line on the edge of the sink, and snorted it.

Cleaned her nose. Cleaned the sink. Looked into the haunted eyes in the mirror. "I'm sorry, Mom," she whispered. Then she gave a sloppy grin and decided she needed just a touch more eye shadow or something.

And the pregnancy test?

She looked down. Mentally registered the result.

She jumped as Aaron pounded on the door and shouted, "Hey! You fall asleep in there?"

"One minute!" she called back. "Jesus!"

She dumped the pregnancy test into the trash and covered it with used facial tissues and panty-liners. She daubed on a touch more lightener under her eyes, put her makeup away and unlocked the door. She flounced out like a fashion model. *Distract him. Make him think everything's fine.*

It obviously worked as Aaron hurried over to her, grabbing her ass with both hands.

"Hey!" she said in mock protest as she retrieved her small party purse that she'd packed earlier and hidden from Aaron. "You want to be late for your folks?"

"Fuck 'em. Got a better idea."

"Your dad pulled me aside after class, you know. He's expecting us."

Aaron shoved her away from him and snorted. "Now we get to it. My dad likes them young. And you knew that, didn't you?"

"What?"

"It's the end of the world and you're trapped with him. Dream or nightmare?"

"Don't be stupid."

He shook his head at her, sucking on his lower lip. "I'm not an idiot. I know you're not happy with me. I just want to know if you'd be happier with him." He reached for her purse.

Jazz hung onto it and gave him a serious look. "I know," she said, "if we're late getting there, he'll cut your off. You want that?"

It got him like she'd known it would and he let go of the purse. "Fuck," he said.

He grabbed her hand and headed for the door and she let him, because all his talk and the buzz of the coke had reignited a stillborn idea she'd had earlier. She just had to get Professor Stoker alone tonight and tell him about his son, what Aaron did to her, then ask him for his help. If he could help warring countries negotiate the release of hostages or whatever, surely he could help Jazz get free.

Surely.

# CHAPTER 5

The Stoker house was across the 520 bridge in a nicer neighborhood of Redmond—forested streets with generous lawns, tasteful money for the well-off, if not truly rich. The sort of place Jazz's parents would have dreamed their whole lives about getting into, she'd thought the first time Jazz had come here with Aaron.

Now, sitting around the Stoker dinner table—a roast beef dinner with mashed potatoes, asparagus, red wine— all she could really think of was how she was going to get out. Because there was no way Professor Stoker was going to help her. Not here. Not tonight. You could see it in...in...

Articulating why she saw that was difficult. She'd found some Percocets in the Stoker bathroom earlier and popped a couple to take the edge off the coke. It was really messing her up.

What she did know was this: it was a full family dinner tonight. Not just her and Aaron on one side with Professor Stoker and his brutal-looking wife, Lindsay, at either end. He was in a pale blue shirt that brought out the blue of his eyes. She wore a pale top with glittery bows and a matching skirt

The other side of the table had Aaron's sister Elizabeth, who must have gotten her looks from Stoker's side and her temperament from who knew where because she was as soft and buxom and kind-eyed as her mother was fierce. Her Spanish husband, Santino, had the same kind eyes. Outlined by his dark Latin brows and lashes, Santino's eyes looked positively dreamy. Unreal. He and Aaron's sister looked like two movies stars—Liz and Santi.

Jazz giggled without showing it (she hoped). Then wondered how Stoker could produce both the wonderful Elizabeth and the cynical, nasty bastard, Aaron.

Cynical, hard, nasty, violent...*and nobody here saw it!* Shit!

"No," Aaron was saying like he was the most reasonable, rational guy. "China doesn't *want* it to work. They want to take over the region. They're afraid if they don't, the US will end up owning everything."

Jesus, how'd they get back onto this subject? You'd think the professor would want to leave his work at the office.

"You're serious?" Elizabeth said. Younger sister but standing up to Aaron because she was raised that way and because she'd married. That gave her the right. "China doesn't have to attack anyone. They've got the biggest economy in the world."

"Which is crumbling," Aaron said. "Right, Dad?"

Ah. Appeal to authority. Jazz understood that. And when she looked lazily at Professor Stoker, she saw him smile back at his son like Aaron was a chip off the old block. Oh, God. That was why he wouldn't believe Jazz. He couldn't.

And just as she thought it, Stoker turned his smile on

her. Trapping her gaze. In her current state it felt like he actually held her head. She couldn't look away as that smile just grew and grew around her. So inappropriate. So...so...

Lindsay-the-wife jumped in with her voice dripping acid. "Yes, Jasmine. Why don't you contribute? Tell us what China will do."

It broke Stoker's trapping smile at least. He shot an annoyed glance at his wife as Jazz mumbled, "Um..."

"She doesn't have to speak if she doesn't want to, darling." Stoker. Overruling the battle-axe.

"But you told me," Lindsay purred, "she spoke up in class today. 'Surprisingly intelligent,' you said."

Then Elizabeth was back at Aaron like the spousal-jealousy show was really irrelevant. "China's not insane. If they invade any of their neighbors..."

Aaron shrugged. "Why stick to neighbors?"

Which finally brought in the gentle Santino. "Oh, my brother. You're bringing out the nuclear thing again?"

"The most recent Chinese subs," Aaron said and stabbed the air to prove how smart he was, "can come within a hundred miles of our shoreline undetected. Tell them, honey."

Whoah. Something she actually knew? Her chance to be smart? If she could make her mouth work...

"Type ninety-eight, Ming class," she found herself reeling out. "Sixteen ballistic missile launch tubes. Short range. And they'll use stealth technology."

"She wrote a paper," Aaron said. Proud boyfriend.

"I got a D." *Fuck you.*

"The prof couldn't handle it."

"He was just being sensible." *Fuck you fuck you.* "How could China ever dare attack the U.S.? That would be crazy." Which was a "Fuck you" to Stoker for his response to her in class earlier. She smiled at him to let him know.

Suddenly her right thigh was clamped by Aaron's hand under the table so hard she almost yelped. She looked at him, eyes wide. His hand gripped further up her thigh, under the hem of her dress, so hard she was sure there'd be bruises. And his eyes said, *Don't you dare contradict me.*

*Yes. Yes. Okay okay.*

"See, little bro?" said Elizabeth, totally missing everything that had just gone on. "You're batting out of your league on this one.

"And you," Aaron retorted, "are just being naïve. You and Mr. Italy there. You believe that deep down everyone just wants love, and the better angels of our nature will save us, right?"

"Don't be a jackass, jackass." Elizabeth took a slug of wine.

"You should sit in on some of Dad's lectures. Altruism and love are aberrations. Suspicion, fear, lust, avarice, the strong over the weak—those are the natural order of things. And the natural order does not change. Tell her, Dad."

Stoker smiled and leaned forward, but Lindsay was having none of it.

"On that note," she said, "let's break for dessert. Raspberry pie. Who doesn't want ice cream with theirs?"

Jazz licked her lips to speak and Aaron's hand reclamped her leg almost at her panty line, like the next one...

Jazz jumped to her feet.

Lindsay looked at her in surprise. "Jasmine?"

"I'm going to help you with the pie," Jazz said.

As she followed the surprised Lindsay into the kitchen, Jazz wondered if Stoker saw the bruises on her inner thigh.

If he was checking her out that closely. If that would disturb or excite him.

*Jesus, Jazz. Get your head on straight.*

Elizabeth jumped into more conversation in the dining room, but Jazz closed the kitchen door behind her, cutting it off. Crazy as it was, Jazz wondered if her true ally here tonight might be the ferocious Lindsay.

Lindsay was pulling out the plates and forks now, clattering them onto the countertop near the sink. She donned some oven mitts and pulled the hot pie from the oven where she'd left it warming, set it beside the plates. Jazz was about to give her a try when Lindsay looked at her and grabbed the chef's knife with way too much enthusiasm.

"Ice cream's in the freezer," Lindsay said. "Top shelf. Scoop's in the drawer to the right of the stove."

"Okay." Jazz stepped carefully to the freezer and breathed easier when Lindsay applied the knife to slicing up the pie. By the time Jazz had the ice cream and scoop, Lindsay was all done and Jazz passed both the ice cream and scoop to her. Anything to get her to put down the knife.

"Mrs. Stoker?"

Lindsay attacked the ice cream now, not acknowledging the question.

"Um, I really appreciate you having me over. And... um...can I ask you a question?"

"Our kids are the biggest gluttons," Lindsay said, dropping a double scoop on what Jazz assumed were Elizabeth's and Aaron's plates.

"It's about Aaron."

Her response was adding a third scoop to the second plate.

"Has he ever...?"

"What?" she snapped. "Robbed a bank? Tortured

kittens? Screwed anything with tits and a shapely ass like yourself?"

Jazz took a step back.

"Oh, grow up, Jasmine. Or can I call you Jazz like Aaron does? I get it. You grew up poor and he gave you a place to live, right? A shoulder to cry on?"

"When my mom died..."

"I don't want to hear it." She turned her back to Jazz as if the words weren't clear enough.

"I'm sorry?"

"I'm not banging you. I don't have to listen."

"It's not that. It's...other stuff."

Lindsay whirled back to her and stepped in so close Jazz could smell her breath. It was sour and desperate. "Listen, Lolita. If you've got problems with your man, deal with it. It's not my problem. Just don't bring my husband into it. *That* would be a very bad mistake."

At that moment, Aaron burst in through the kitchen door and stopped, looking with raised eyebrows between the two women.

Lindsay smiled and turned for the plates. "Let's take out the pie and ice cream, shall we?"

Aaron tailed Jazz as she followed Lindsay out with plates and served them around. As she served Elizabeth, the young woman's hand covered hers and gave her a quick squeeze. Jazz looked into Elizabeth's eyes, shocked to see an encouraging smile there.

So *that's* who she should have gone to.

Then Aaron was hustling her back to her seat and holding it out for her like he wanted to play more thigh-grab under the table. Jazz shook he head and grabbed her small handbag.

"Actually, I don't feel well. I think I need to use the bathroom."

She hurried off, almost tripping over the cat that had come from nowhere to wrap itself around her ankles.

"Sorry!" she said as the tabby darted away. "Sorry sorry sorry."

Ten seconds later she was in the hall bathroom. She closed and locked the door behind her, then turned and held onto the sink for dear life, taking deep gulping breaths. She thought the Percocet would calm her down, make this whole thing manageable. But now her heart was pounding and her anxiety level was going through the roof.

She could handle despair, feeling trapped and helpless. It was what she deserved. It was what her father's low expectations had programmed into her from the time she was little. But then her mother's hope for her... And Randy appearing like a carrot-topped knight in shining armor... And Elizabeth's hand squeeze and smile...

Oh God! She couldn't handle hope when it couldn't get her anywhere. There was nowhere to go. No one she could be who could be free and independent and...*worth* something.

She slapped water on her face then stared at horror at how she'd messed up her makeup. Grabbing her bag, she started rifling through it for some mascara and lipstick.

*Bang! Bang! Bang!*

She dropped her bag and spun around to hear Aaron's voice murmuring with deadly calm through the door. "Better not be using, you little twat."

She held up a hand at the too-thin door between them. "Go away."

"I mean it," Aaron purred. "You're not back out here in five, I'm coming in."

She heard his footsteps retreat.

"Oh Jesus. Of fuck." What to do?

She dug into her handbag again and came up with her cracked cell phone. It showed she had three voice messages from the Women's Emergency Services. Damn it! She'd never felt it buzz. Maybe that much of the phone was broken now.

She tapped and poked at the screen but couldn't get it to open. Then, surprisingly, it was dialing back the Women's Emergency Services. Well okay. *Okay.*

They picked up!

CHAPTER 6

JAZZ HELD the cracked phone to her ear, about to speak, when she heard the familiar canned message: "We're sorry. Everyone's away from the phone right now or dealing with other callers. Please leave your name and number and we'll call you back as soon as possible."

"Shit shit shit!" Jasmine breathed over top of it. Then the beep sounded in her ear. "I can't do this anymore," she said into the phone. "He's going to kill me."

Then she stabbed at the phone again and again until it apparently hung up. She sniffed, wiped her nose, shoved the phone back in her bag and slipped out the bathroom door.

But she wasn't going back to the dining room table. No way.

She swayed on the balls of her feet, looking over at the front door, then to her right where the dining room was...*with a full view of the front door.* But they wouldn't be looking that way, would they? Wouldn't be expecting her to just leave.

So she took a deep breath and did her best ghost run to

the door, opening it silently, carefully, slipping out, and closing it just as carefully behind her.

Then she just walked. She didn't know where she was going to go. Maybe not back to school. Maybe out of state. Maybe out of country. Somewhere. Anywhere...

The front door of the Stoker house burst open behind her and she looked back to see Aaron standing on the front step, looking around, spotting her. "Hey!" he shouted.

Jazz ran.

But so did Aaron, and he wasn't wearing a tight dress and heels.

He caught her before she'd made it past the next house. Grabbed her roughly by the arms and pulled her back into his chest so his mouth was right by her ear, pressing her head painfully sideways.

"Tonight, when we get home..."

He didn't finish, though, as a second voice called out, "Jasmine, are you all right?"

Elizabeth! Her rescuer after all! Jazz tried to turn but Aaron hadn't loosened his grip one bit.

"She's fine!" he called back to his sister. "Allergic reaction to something she ate. She just needed some fresh air."

Then Aaron's grip suddenly loosened so that Jazz could turn around. Ah, there was why. Not only Elizabeth had come out of the Stoker house. Her husband had followed her out. And Professor Stoker. And Lindsay, though the Stoker matriarch was merely standing, annoyed, on the front step while the others were actually walking out onto the dark little cul-de-sac towards Jazz and Aaron.

As Professor Stoker and the others reached her and Jazz, Stoker looked at her closely, then his son. "Should you take her to a hospital?"

And before Aaron could come up with a good lie, the

crowd got even bigger. The neighbor's house Jazz had almost made it past—obviously undergoing a renovation from the tarps over part of the roof and the big construction-debris bin in the front driveway—had spilled out its residents. Coming towards Stoker was a burly-looking man in his thirties. Behind him on the front step stood what had to be the man's young wife. She held the hand of their young girl, spotted Lindsay and waved. Lindsay waved back ironically.

The burly-looking man, too soft to be a fireman, but clearly used to taking charge, hitched up his jeans as he stopped near them.

"Hey, Scott," he addressed Stoker. "What's wrong? Can I help?"

Stoker barely looked at him. "No, I think we've got it, Jeff."

"You sure? You know my wife's a nurse. Always looks after our daughter, Annie, there. I'm sure she could—"

"Really. Thank you."

The burly man, Jeff, nodded, but his face looked flushed in the dark. "Scott, listen to me. I insist. I know you guys aren't big into the whole neighbors-helping-neighbors thing, but you know there's a *value* to people working together. And I don't want to put you on the spot, but when you close yourself off like this, when you close your family off from everyone else, it's almost an aggressive act. A hostile rejection, you understand? And I know you don't want to do that. So why don't you let my wife take a look at your girl there and—"

Stoker finally faced him fully with all the authority, Jazz figured, that came from addressing university classes, policy wonks, city and country officials, and whomever.

"Jeff? Let me put it to you this way: fuck off. The answer's no. Go away."

There was a beat when Jazz wondered if the much-bigger Jeff would physically pound the smaller and older, but clearly more mentally powerful, Stoker. Jeff finally wilted, shrugged like it wasn't a big deal, and retreated to his wife and child.

Stoker turned to Jazz, Aaron, Elizabeth and her husband, Santino. "Can we go back inside now?"

Jazz looked at Elizabeth. If she could be sure Elizabeth would support her... But her husband was pointing out the stars overhead and murmuring in her ear. Elizabeth was giggling. And Stoker clearly believed his son could do no wrong. And where was Jazz going to go, anyway? Walk to a bus stop? Aaron would follow her. Call a cop? Aaron would tell them she was a drug user. Make the cop test her right there. Jazz had no money to speak of, a broken phone, and a boyfriend who was just itching for an excuse to beat her up again.

"Sure," Aaron said. "Honey? Feeling better?"

Jazz nodded. "Yeah."

They escorted her back to the house.

On the front step, though, just as Aaron was about to drag her in after Elizabeth and Santino, her cell phone buzzed in her handbag.

"What the—?" said Aaron.

But Jazz had it out in her hand and up to her ear, holding a hand up to Aaron as if it were perfectly reasonable for her to be able to take a call privately. With Stoker there, Aaron could only give her a smile that promised payback later.

A woman spoke on the phone with a tone that was

strong and sure. "This is Women's Emergency Services. Is this Jasmine Kazmi?"

"Yes, but...I can't talk right now."

"Okay, sweetie," the voice said. "The guy you're afraid of, is he there right now?"

"Yes."

"Then just tell me where you are right now. Are you at home in the Mallory Apartments?"

"No. 555 Crestview. Yes, bring the cake here any time."

She pulled it from her ear and stabbed at the Hang Up button twice before it registered.

Aaron grabbed for the phone. "What kind of bullshit...?"

"Aaron!" Stoker said and put a hand on his son's arm.

Aaron dropped his arm and Jazz quickly put her phone back in her handbag. Then they were through the door and Jazz felt a surge of panic. If Aaron pulled out her phone and saw who'd called, he'd take her out of the house immediately. Then, whether he took her back to the apartment directly or not, he'd do whatever he could to make sure she never talked to the women's service people again. Or the cops. Maybe not to anyone.

Jazz half-curled over like she was going to vomit. "I need to use the washroom again."

And without looking to see if once again Aaron was only restrained by his father's presence, Jazz lurched for the bathroom door. She saw Aaron and Stoker head to the dining room.

But rather than go into the bathroom, Jazz crept further down the hallway. She had to hide. How long would it take the cops to get here? If she could just hide and wait. Hide and...

She tried the door on the right. The master bedroom.

King size bed so Stoker and his wife can sleep well away from each other. En suite bathroom and walk-in closet. Too easy to find her in there.

She closed the door, took another couple steps and tried the door on the left.

Stairs down. The basement. She clicked on the light and slipped in. Closed the door behind her. The steps went straight down to what looked like an unfinished room with concrete walls and floor. As she crept a few quiet steps down, she could see junk. Shelving. Gross. But probably lots of good places to hide. She'd find one then come back up and turn out the light.

She was about halfway down when she heard the click of the door opening behind her.

She froze. Turned. Looked up.

But it wasn't Aaron. It was his father. Stoker. Jazz almost expected him to laugh and say, "Caught you!" But Stoker said nothing. He just closed the door quietly behind him then started down towards her, carrying something in his right hand.

A baseball bat!

Oh shit.

Jazz turned and started a stumbling run down the stairs, only to be lifted off her feet with a *CRACK!* that made everything go black.

CHAPTER 7

SHE SQUIRMED in a hot void with Aaron's face, close and distorted and shouting at her. "You think you can leave me?! You think you can just get up and run away?!"

While behind him somewhere, something thudded over and over like someone was trying to break down a door. A muffled "Hey! Hey!"

Trying to rescue her? She began to thrash in panic, gasping and screaming.

And suddenly Aaron's angry face resolved into Stoker's crazed, sweaty one in the flickering hiss of a gas lantern light as he struggled to hold her down. No other light. It was Hell! She was in Hell!

"Jasmine!" Stoker shouted at her. "It's okay! Stop screaming!"

She screamed louder, louder, her face pulsing with blood...and everything spun to black.

CHAPTER 8

THE NEXT TIME Jazz swam back to consciousness, she heard the hiss of the gas lantern again, but it was further away from her this time, over on the floor by a gap between two steel-bolted shelving units. Basement? Was she in a basement? No windows anywhere. Just that lantern.

Stoker squatted near it with a notebook, apparently taking inventory of whatever was on the two long, tightly-packed shelving units that bisected the basement. Stoker still wore the dress pants and pale blue, button-down shirt he'd worn at the family dinner. They were dirtier now, though, the shirt sticking to him, the knee of one of his pant legs ripped.

And the air... It was so hot and rancid with her own body odor that Jazz felt like she was burning up. Her party dress felt soaked through. Sweat trickled into her eyes.

She went to wipe it and realized she couldn't. Her wrists were bound above her head to the steel corners of the cot she lay on. Or narrow bed? It had a thin mattress covered by a sheet and that wasn't the kind of light tubing she remembered from her childhood camping trips. A thin, lumpy pillow was bunched under her head. Her ankles were spread and bound to the bottom corners. Sharp and tight.

She felt a moment of panic as she pulled against them but dropped all motion and closed her eyes when Stoker obviously heard the squeaking of the springs and looked up.

Through her eyelashes, she watched him stand and walk over to her. He stood near her waist, looking down at her, his expression too shadowed to read. Finally he leaned down towards her face and she saw a glint of a necklace chain inside his shirt.

He checked the pulse in Jazz's neck. His hand smelled of gasoline. After a pause, he slid his hand down to her breast...

She jerked and he drew back. She fluttered her eyes open.

"You're awake," he said. Asking if she'd *been* awake?

She shook her head like she was really just coming to. "I'm... You're...Professor Stoker. Why am I tied down?"

"Safety. For both of us. Trust me, you were unsettled the last time you woke up."

"I'm not now. Please untie me?" She said it as a question because she'd learned from her time with Aaron that you couldn't be too assertive of your rights. You had to recognize the power of an alpha male so they'd 1) not punish you and 2) maybe consider your question as something they should take seriously.

Which seemed to work here. Stoker smiled down at her. "I will. Maybe. After we get a few things straight."

"No, please. I get scared, phobic, about restraints." Especially when men grabbed at her breasts and had her locked down here for...how long? How *long?*

"Take a deep breath," he said.

"UNTIE ME!"

Then she struggled, forgetting what she knew about deference and personal safety, just angry and insanely scared. She screamed. Someone had to hear. Jerked at her restraints so they cut into her bare wrists and ankles. Screamed again. And again. Until she was dizzy. Hoarse.

Until she finally subsided into a croaky wheeze, staring at Stoker, at the ceiling, at the shadowed walls and rows of shelves that stretched across one side of the basement room —two across, then two behind that, and maybe two more still? Loaded with provisions like he planned to keep her down here for months. Years. Forever.

She tried to snarl at him to hide her tears.

"See, now there's the problem," he said.

"*What?* What's the fucking problem?"

He gestured at the space around them. "We're in a precarious situation here and you're still caught in a fear state. Now, I get the feeling I could probably harness that by hitting you."

He raised a hand and Jazz's well-trained defense mechanisms made her flinch back as far as she could on the cot.

But he didn't strike her. And something told her she had to push that, at whatever it was that made him hold back from hitting her.

"You *already* hit me!" she said. "On the head! And tied me up! How long have I been out?"

"Two days, but—"

Two days... And nobody had looked for her? What had Stoker told Aaron? Did everyone think she'd just run away? So nobody would be looking for her now. Nobody ever would. Oh God...

Her eyes started to fill and she squeezed them shut.

"Jasmine..." Stoker began.

She sprung open her eyes and tried to lung at him. "What have you done with me for two days, you sonofabitch! You—"

"You had a concussion! And no food or water!"

"—knock me out. You tie me up. You hold me here and...and then you..."

It was too much for her system and she felt herself spinning down to black again. Which she couldn't do, because what would he do to her now that she'd defied him?

It was her last thought before she lost consciousness.

Jazz woke up, groggy, to the sound of more thumping like someone pounding at a door. Muffled keening. It stopped. Heavy breathing.

Not just a dream then.

There was still the oppressive heat and still the only light was from the gas camping lantern that was sitting on the edge of the small table near other side of the room. She thought she could smell the gas. Her mouth tasted like moldy paper. Stoker was nowhere in sight.

Jazz tried to sit up but was still bound. Her wrists. Her ankles. It looked like they were being held by plastic zip ties. Could she break them? She thought she'd seen a YouTube video once where they showed you how.

But when she tugged hard on a wrist or tried kicking a foot, all it brought were sharp jabs of pain as the plastic bit into her skin. And she felt weak as a baby. Two days with no food or drink, Stoker had said. On top of the drugs. On top of weeks of poor diet and rotten sleep.

She was in sucky shape to be planning a prison break.

But if Stoker was actually not here right now...

Even as she thought it, from the direction from which she'd heard the heavy breathing, up the stairs, she realized, came a clumping sound and Stoker appeared. She went still and watched him through her eyelashes as he trudged over to the far corner from her cot. A minute later he returned with a cordless drill, a two-foot canvas sack clanked and rattled, and two wooden 2x4's. Not even glancing at her, he grabbed the gas light and climbed with it back up the stairs. She watched until his feet vanished past the ceiling.

Stopped. There was a clattering. Then drilling sounds. Pounding.

He wasn't gone then. Maybe had never been gone, even while she'd been trying to break free. And when he came back down...

She used the few moments of being unobserved to figure out as much as she could about the place she was trapped in.

A basement, obviously. Was it the one in the Stoker house or had he taken her somewhere else? Most of this basement was deep in shadows with lantern light up the stairs, but she could put together the pictures from what she'd seen before Stoker had gone up the stairs.

The stairs. They looked kind of like what she remembered coming down before he hit her.

And down here? The walls and floors were unfinished cement. She remembered that. The ceiling? It wasn't cement, she could see. Wood rafters, it looked like, but packed with insulation.

The line of shelves she'd seen earlier were stocked with supplies, so Stoker had obviously planned to use this place as some kind of bomb shelter or place to store kidnap victims. So maybe she wasn't the first? How did he manage that in his own house?

And what she couldn't figure out was why there was a second cot on the other side of the room, near the table. She hadn't registered it consciously before, but now she could see its dark shadow and remembered. Like hers, it looked solid, with a thin mattress, a pillow, no covers. But it somehow looked slept on. And there was something like a radio on top of the table, too. And a notebook? A pen...

The scrap of Stoker's footsteps on the stairs sent a surge of adrenaline through her. Was this where he made her pay for her backtalk yesterday? Had he just been waiting for her to wake up?

She considered feigning sleep again but realized again how parched her mouth was. Her whole body felt like it was drying and shriveling up.

So when Stoker descended far enough with the lantern that she could see his scuffed shoes and dirty slacks, then his hands carrying his tool bag and drill but no longer the 2x4's, she could barely contain herself.

She let him get to the far corner and put down his tools and bag.

"Water?" she croaked.

Stoker startled and spun around like he'd almost forgotten she was there. "My god, yes."

He hurried to a central shelf and drew her a cup of water from the spigot of a large, horizontal water bottle.

He grabbed one of the basement's two chairs and dragged it over beside her cot. Sat there and held the cup to Jazz's lips. She had to crane her head up to be able to drink and still ended up spilling a quarter of it down cheeks, down her neck, into the top of her dress. She saw his eyes following it, but she was too thirsty and desperate to take another stab at getting him to free her hands right now.

When she emptied the first cup, she gasped, "More."

Stoker nodded, stood, and came back a moment later with another filled cup. "Slowly," he said, and held the cup to her lips, this time supporting her head with free hand so her quivering neck muscles didn't shake his target so much.

After the second cup, she felt almost human again. Almost.

"Food?" she said. As a question. Because if there was one thing she'd learned from living with Aaron, it was that abusers responded better to questions than demands.

Stoker nodded, stood, and went to the shelves again. He returned with a chocolate pudding cup and a small spoon. Her saliva went wild when he ripped off the cover and the smell rolled into her nose. It was all she could do to not inhale the pudding off the spoon when he brought it close.

"Go easy," he said. "You don't want to get sick."

Which made Jazz want to laugh in his face or bite him or something. Warning her about eating too fast when he'd knocked her out, tied her down, was feeding her like a helpless child...

She nodded and kept eating.

When she was done, it was enough. Her stomach was knotting up. She lay her head back down on the cot's lumpy pillow and looked at Stoker. "What were you doing?" she asked.

"What? Where?" He licked out the last bits of pudding from inside the cup. His tongue dipping into it like a snake, over and over, like he wanted her to see it.

"Up at the door. Why didn't people hear me scream?"

Stoker crumpled the emptied pudding cup. "We'll get

to that later." His tongue dipped into the edge of the crumpled cup.

This was a nightmare. The latest of a run of them. Jazz's whole life. She could feel her thoughts starting to circle, spiraling downwards. "I need my purse."

"Your what?"

"My purse. My leather bag. I need the stuff from my bag."

"Meaning your drugs? A small bag of cocaine and a bunch of loose pills that look like they came from my wife's stash or opiods. A bad combination. Could make you sick, delusional, maybe even paranoid."

"It's not your business, Professor. They're mine. Bring them to me. And untie me."

The look he gave her made her instantly wish she could swallow the words again. A command when she should have asked. A bad tone of voice. Aaron would have struck her, hard and fast, across her face. No expression. Or maybe even sympathy in his eyes. Like he was sorry she was so stupid and had to learn how to behave. But she'd learned. She knew she was stupid. Stupid for staying with him, but even more sure he'd find her and hurt her more if she tried to leave. Because that was how the world worked, right? Evil latched onto you and you couldn't shake it off. Even if you ran away from one form of it, there was no real escape.

Ever.

"You can call me Scott," her captor, her new face of evil now purred at her. "And there's nothing to bring you anymore, Jasmine. I poured your drugs down the drain. They weren't helping you. Illegal substances never do."

He ran a finger along her jaw line as he said it, like he was talking about *her* being an illegal substance, with a nudge-nudge, wink-wink. And despite her inner caution voice screaming at her, she couldn't help herself.

She shook her chin to throw off his finger. "Fuck you! You arrogant asshole! You condescending, kidnapping pervert! *I needed those!* They were *mine!*"

He grabbed her chin. "No. You see, that's not the game we're playing anymore—smart-but-troubled drug addict sleeping with my son. That role is over. Everything's changed. Do you understand? You can't go back."

And even though she knew she was caught, trapped by this new evil, the crazy part inside her that her mother always told her was a wild animal couldn't take it, couldn't accept. She snarled and snapped her teeth at him, hoping to catch a finger but just getting air,

She roared in frustration and it caught her up like a wild wave until she was screaming. She spat at him. Pulled against her restraints until she felt like her ankles and wrists were going to be sliced apart or the springs under her were going to snap. Shook and screamed some more. Until...

She fell back hard against her pillow and stared at the dark ceiling. Breathed in and out. So hot. So caught. Oh fuck.

"Okay," she said.

"Okay what?" said Stoker.

She realized he still sat on the chair beside her cot. He'd barely pulled away during her epic struggle. Like he knew just how close he could get. Just how far her writhing head and body could reach.

"Really. What?" he pressed her. "You've had enough to eat and drink? Or okay, you understand that things have changed?"

Breathe, Jasmine. Just... "Okay, I'm here. With you. For now. Untie me."

"Hm." He looked at her, up and down. Clearly liked doing that. "Unfortunately, you don't understand what's happened or the situation we're in."

"Really?" *Fucker.* "Tell my *your* version of what happened."

"Brace yourself."

Stoker sat back in his chair, considering her again before he spoke. And when he did, it was like a well-rehearsed lecture. Like telling his class about the events that led up to the formation of ISIL—boom, boom, boom.

"Three days ago, you and Aaron came over for a dinner party. Aaron's sister, her husband, me and my wife, Lindsay. Yes?"

Checking that the class was listening. Jazz nodded her head.

"At one point," Stoker continued, "you ran out of the house. When you came back in, you went to the bathroom again. Aaron was very upset. So I excused myself just in time to see you sneak into the basement. You looked up. You saw me."

"You shut the door behind you," Jazz said. "Trapping me."

"To talk with you privately. To find out what was going on with you and Aaron."

"You were carrying a baseball bat!"

He'd leaned forward slightly as he talked and Jazz could

swear the sweaty excitement pouring off him. But now his teaching mode kicked in again. Maybe an automatic reflex when he sensed his female students were catching the creeper vibe.

"Observant, Ms. Kazmi. I was carrying the bat Aaron used in the Triple A league when he was ten. It was to be a demonstrative prop. To tell you how much he meant to me. It's over there, against the last shelf.

Jazz craned her neck up. Saw it. Noted its position for when she finally managed to get free of this bed. Then she let her head drop back. "Right. Sure. Okay. Then what walloped me over the head?"

"Probably the metal support pole by the stairs. I think you were thrown into it head first."

"By you? Why would—?"

"By the blast wave."

Jazz blinked. "The what?"

"The blast wave from what I'm assuming was a thermonuclear device probably detonated some three hundred feet above the city."

Jazz stared at him. His face wasn't twitching. Wasn't even holding the sardonic smirk he sometimes used in class to tell his students he expected them to challenge him. No, Stoker's face was just relaxed and watching her, like he was waiting for her to catch up. But come on. Surely he didn't expect...

"An atomic bomb," she said at last, voice dripping. "A... seriously? An atomic bomb?"

"Actually, as I said, almost certainly a thermonuclear device. You should recall from that paper you said you did, atom bombs are strictly fission devices. Modern nukes use fission to start a fusion reaction. Far more powerful. And if China or Russia were going to—"

"Stop! You actually want me to believe we were hit with a nuclear bomb. That's why we're down here?"

"I'm guessing the South China Sea talks did not go well."

Jazz stared at him. Still the calm, waiting face. Like he truly expected her to just accept it. But, like, you know, which was more likely? Nukes hitting the US, which had never happened in over a half-century of threats, or that a man who'd produced an abusive, manipulative monster of a son happened to be a psychopath himself?

She laughed in his face. Felt the laughter grip her in a kind of braying against the panic so it was a while before she calmed down.

"And that, I'm guessing," said Stoker when she finally quieted, "was because of the irony. You suggest this in class, then you're one of the few who survive an actual such attack."

"Sure. That's what it is. I'm all about the irony."

"Hm."

Jazz saw a reaction flicker in his eyes and her inner voice that had been learning how to deal with psychopaths, *Don't push it*. But come on! Aaron might have beaten her, but he'd never insulted her intelligence. Her will, maybe, but not her understanding of how the world worked. "Prove it," she said.

"Pardon me?"

"Let me go. Show me outside."

This time his considering gaze was just on her eyes, like he was trying to read her thoughts, her will, her planning. Except there was nothing there to read, really. She had no thoughts except that she didn't believe him. Her only will and plan was to get free of this cot. She didn't really believe she could get free of Stoker himself.

Even as the animal inside her, which had finally re-awakened just enough to make stabs at getting away from Aaron, growled that she *could* get free. Maybe. Somehow? Why?

Because Stoker hadn't beaten her. Because he was playing mind games like he wanted something else from her. Because Jazz knew she was weak, that she'd let herself collapse for so long she was barely a puddle of nothing. But she was smart. She knew she was smart. And if the professor was going to make this all about brains, a battle of wits, then maybe somehow she had a chance.

Stoker shifted suddenly and Jazz's guts froze. She was wrong. He was going to beat her.

But he just calmly reached down to the gas lantern he'd set on the floor near her cot and he lifted it up near his face. In its hissing light, Jazz could now see red marks splashed down the left side of Stoker's neck and chin.

"When I looked outside, after the blast, after I picked myself up and dragged you to this cot, everything was on fire. The air. I could hardly breathe. And most of the house was simply gone. No second floor. Just blazing sticks for walls. No...kitchen, dining room..."

It trailed off.

Jazz waited. There was something pregnant in Stoker's eyes. Like he truly had seen something like this, in his imagination at least, and it raised the logical consequence of loss. Of his family. Of everyone he knew up there. His job. His future.

He could have been a great actor. Jazz almost bought it.

"Let me see it," she said.

Stoker snapped out of it and shook his head. Put the lantern back on the floor. "When I understood what had to have happened, I came back in here and sealed up the door.

I may already be dead from radiation poisoning, long term. Or not. But I will not expose you or myself to it again without good reason. Not until the fires have time to burn out. And there's actually someplace to go."

"Someplace..."

Stoker waved his hand vaguely at the shelves of supplies. "We've got about ten days worth of water. Double that if we ration it. Radiation should be less by then, but we'll probably have to hike ten or twenty miles out of the blast zone to find anything safe. Or alive."

Jazz gave an involuntary gasp.

Stoker nodded. "There aren't a lot of Seattle houses with deep basements. And the number of people who happened to be in their basement, with provisions, when the blast hit..." He glanced back at the table near the other cot. "I'm not picking up any radio signals."

Again Jazz found herself falling into the performance. So good. But all she had to do to bring herself back was tug on her ankle and wrist restraints. They *hurt*.

"So that's your version," she said.

"Yes, Ms. Kazmi," he sighed. "That's my version."

"Which is fundamentally untestable if you won't let me see for myself. Could I listen at the door? Hear the fires burning?"

"The way I've sealed up the door, you can't hear anything. And the only reason we're alive is the thickness of the concrete walls and heavily insulated ceiling."

Of course. "So I just have to trust you."

"Yes." A simple fact.

"And fuck you?" Had to be said, Jazz thought as she held her breath. Next step in the game: bring out the stakes. See how he reacts. Does he cover? Does he divert? Does he get right down to it?

"What?"

Okay. A stall. Nothing. Give him permission for admission. "Because there's just the two of us now, right? Maybe the only two people left alive for hundreds of miles."

"I didn't say that."

Pull him in. "But you've got no radio signals. We don't know how many bombs dropped. If all the major centers were wiped out, even the people in the interior are going to lose power and supplies. There's going to be panic, refugees, violence, starvation..."

"I... Maybe."

Come on. Pin him down. "That leaves just me and serendipitously-prepared-you to rely on each other. Become the new Adam and Eve. Pretty much what you've set up here, isn't it?"

Ouch. Too much. She hadn't been able to stop the sarcasm from creeping in. And of course he'd heard it. Of course. So what now? Back off? Let it lie?

"Ms. Kazmi..."

*No.* She had to know now what to prepare herself for. "Shut up, *Scott*. You've wanted to fuck me from the first time you knew your son was doing it. Isn't that right?"

"No, that's—"

"Bullshit. He told me as much. Warned me about you. Warned me you like to seduce your prettiest young students."

"You think highly of yourself."

"I'm here! You know what we call a prof who can't take his eyes off his female students? A creeper. A sick, damaged pervert. I bet everyone at the university knows you're one."

Then Jazz saw Stoker do the strangest thing. Rather than leap to his own defense or slap her or walk away, he began drumming the fingers of his right hand against his leg.

Was he holding back from hitting her? Was it his way of handling extreme stress, like Jazz snorting coke or popping meth? Jesus, what?

"Now you're just being insulting," Stoker said with an almost too-even voice. "I was never anything but professional with my students."

Okay, pivot. "And you're so in love with your wife. She made that clear."

His fingers stopped drumming. "Was. I was."

"How many years ago, Professor? When did the romance between the two of you fizzle into routine, then into indifference, and finally turn the corner into disgust? Hunh?"

He bared his teeth, his face red. "You heartless... My wife of twenty-six years is dead. Along with my son, my daughter."

"Says you."

"Yes. Says me."

Jazz opened her mouth to retort but Stoker jerked up a hand and she flinched back. Here it was. Here it was...

He struggled. She could smell the sharp tang of his rage. She could see the end all at once, with him losing it and her, unable even to cover herself, writhing back and forth under his blows, feeling her kidneys collapse, her ribs crack, the blood spray from her nose, fill her mouth with hot gagging...

Then Stoker somehow regained his self-control. Almost too much. When he spoke, it was like a ghost speaking, the words echoing through the shadows of the basement from another existence.

"Ms. Kazmi," the ghost said. "Jasmine. I know this is a lot to take in. I've had three days, and that was with visceral proof of what happened. And I...understand why it must be easier to believe I'm some kind of mad rapist than that we've suffered a doomsday event. I get that. It's Occam's Razor—the simplest explanation. But it's the wrong one."

He brought his hand to his mouth. Covering a laugh? Or holding in the horror he had to speak? Because that's what this was—a horror. How dare he know what she was thinking, acknowledge it, and then tell her it was smart and reasonable but wrong? How dare he make the ridiculous sound...plausible?

"Now, believe it or not," Stoker said, "it's actually ten p.m. Bedtime. So I'm going to get ready to sleep. You can do the same or just think over everything I've said. And if you're able to start facing the reality of the situation—that Aaron's not coming to get you ever again, that you're stuck with me now, here in this basement—then in the morning I'll free your wrists, at least, so you can eat breakfast like a human being. It will be your choice."

So saying, he picked up the gas lantern from the floor again, stood, and walked back towards the other cot, dragging the chair behind him and putting it up to the table with the radio, the lamp on the table.

As she watched, he turned back towards her and slowly unbuttoned his shirt. Took it off. Like a crazy strip tease. And she saw he was buff. Old man buff. His midriff was thick and fleshy, but he'd built up his chest and arms. Pushups? Barbells?

The golden light from the gas lantern on the table seemed to reach out and caress his sweaty pecs and the necklace nestled between them...

His hands went to the top of his pants and stopped. He looked over and saw her watching.

"Think it all through, Jasmine. All of it. Logically. And remember what I said—if you can just accept the reality of what's happened here, tomorrow I'll take off at least those stupid wrist ties."

*Ohhhhh*, she wanted to growl at him. *Don't you dare do that. Don't you dare feed me crazy lies, push to make them sound real, then offer bait, a reward, if I start to swallow them. Don't. You. Dare.*

But she said nothing. And just as he reached to undo his pants with one hand, the other found the switch on the lantern and...

The light went out.

"Psst!"

The sound seemed at first the part of a dream. Then Jazz opened her eyes to the utter blackness of the basement and heard it again.

"Psst!"

Jazz looked around, then down to the foot of her cot and saw who was making the sound. Elizabeth Stoker, the professor's daughter, Aaron's sister. Somehow she carried light with her. Not inside her. She wasn't glowing. She was just...lit. Even though nothing else in the basement, but for the foot of the cot that Elizabeth sat on, was visible.

Dream then. Okay.

"You know," Elizabeth said, "he was a really great dad. A little condescending at times, very demanding, but when he laughed... God, I loved his laugh."

Jazz looked to where Stoker's cot had to be in the darkness and was vaguely surprised to see it was somehow lit too. Stoker was curled up on top of it wearing only his boxer shorts, looking peaceful. An innocent babe.

"Was he ethical?" Jazz asked.

"Oh, yeah. Well, mostly. I know he used to smoke pot, cheat on his taxes sometimes. And on Mom once, I think."

"With a student?"

Elizabeth shrugged. "I don't know. Just someone, Mom says."

Jazz looked back towards Stoker and realized another person had joined them. It was Stoker's wife, Lindsay, circling Stoker where he lay on his cot. And because nothing beyond the cot and Stoker and Lindsay were visible, it created the oddest visual of a human shark circling a sleeping prey in ice-black waters.

As Jazz watched, Lindsay darted in to sit by Stoker's torso. She pulled out a hunting knife from somewhere and held it the edge of the blade up against his throat. The knife made a metallic keening noise, like it was alive and wanted blood.

Jazz held her breath.

"Such a big mistake," said a new voice. Santino. He leaned out of the darkness to wrap his arms around his wife, Elizabeth. She snuggled back into him.

"Mm-hm."

"'Cause when you get right down to it," he said, "there's nothing more important than having someone to hold onto, am I right?"

His hands had crept up to Elizabeth's breasts as he talked and when he fondled them and brushed the nipples through her shirt, Elizabeth sighed and turned her face back to meet his lips in a kiss so erotic that Jazz felt herself grow wet, her breasts tingling.

She squirmed against her bonds as the married couple's kiss just kept getting wetter and deeper. "Guys..." she said.

And Aaron was suddenly behind her head. "That make you uncomfortable, Jazzy baby?"

"I…"

He leaned down so his breath was right beside her face. "Or are you just wishing" – his hands started running lightly down the sides of her body – "that you could join in with your eager beaver?"

His right hand cupped her between her legs. She gasped as a wave of excitement shot through her whole body, then gasped again as he fingered her. "Is that what *he* wants?" she said.

Elizabeth and Santino were sliding to the floor, shedding their clothes in a frenzy, but Jazz lost track of them as Aaron grabbed her chin, turning her face towards him as he walked around the side of the cot and straddled her. "It's what I want," he said, and removed his shirt.

Hard abs and a hard rod between his legs.

*No!* "You can't control me anymore," she said and tried to shift him off. "You're dead."

He grinned. "Says who?"

"Then why didn't you hear me? Why didn't you come for me when I screamed?"

From across the room, Lindsay's face snapped sideways at her. "Oh, boo-hoo. Poor little twat got herself stuck with the big bad wolf and wants someone to rescue her."

"Maybe I didn't hear you," said Aaron. He ran his hands up under her shirt. Found her breasts. Squeezed.

She yelped. "He soundproofed the door."

Pinched the nipples. "Or you're not where you think you are."

Before Jazz could respond, Lindsay did it for her, shrieking, "You son of a bitch!" She grabbed her husband's head by the hair, lifted it up, and dragged a knife across Stoker's throat. Blood sprayed in every direction, even spattering Jazz's face, making her…

CHAPTER 12

*W*AKE UP*!*

Jazz's eyes shot open to utter blackness.

"It's a different basement!"

Through the darkness from across the room, came a groan and shuffle. Then a clinking sound of metal and glass, a hiss of gas, the scratch of a match. Jazz squinted at the tiny light then reared back, blinking, as the mantle of the lantern caught and flared on. Stoker dialed it down and squinted across the basement at her.

"What?" he said.

Jazz looked wildly around her. Was this truly the place she tried to hide out during that disastrous dinner party? She'd only had a brief look, but if it wasn't... It made so much sense.

"Different basement," she said. "I went into your basement, you knocked me out, then you went back to the party and told everyone I left. And when everyone was asleep, you went back, dragged me out, stuck me in the trunk of your car, and drove me to this place. It's on the edge of town or out in the forest, right? Somewhere you planned to put me all along. Or someone. It just happened to be me."

Stoker shook his head tiredly. "Jasmine. Jazz..."

"Don't call me that! Don't you dare call me that!"

"Ms. Kazmi, okay? You were having a nightmare."

Jazz tugged up her fists as far as she could and shook the cot. "*This* is the nightmare! I've been fucking kidnapped by a psycho rapist who's going to kill me!"

Stoker sighed and swung his feet off the bed to the floor so he was sitting. "If I wanted to rape you or kill you, don't you think I would have done it by now?"

"Unless..." The thought hit her like a gut punch and her body consciousness went spiraling down into that place between her legs that Aaron had abused so much. "Unless you have already. I was unconscious for three days!"

Again Stoker's tired head shake. "For the love of rational thought, go back to sleep. We'll hash this out in the morning."

The thought made panic jump into Jazz's throat. "No! There's no chance of light. How do I even know what time it is?" Had to keep talking. Stave off the darkness. "Do you leave when I go to sleep, then sneak back in with supplies for you game? You're controlling me. Everything I see and hear and feel. This is sick, professor. Sick and sadistic! It's—"

"Hey!" Stoker held up his wrist, pointing to the watch she now noticed he wore. "My watch still works. At least until its battery dies. As long as I'm not somehow off by twelve hours, it's...three-thirty a.m."

He reached for the lamp and Jazz yelled out, "I don't care! My arms and legs hurt. My wrists. I'm hungry. And I need to pee! Right now!"

Stoker grimaced. "Of course you do. All right. Just a minute."

With more groans, he rose and reached down to grab and pull on his dress pants. He had a hunting knife in a sheath attached to its waistband, Jazz noted. Wildly incongruous, but some part of her must have registered it before. That's why it turned up in Lindsay's hand in her dream.

Stoker finished doing up his pants, then walked to the nearest shelf, grabbed a bunch of fresh zip-ties and jammed them into his pocket. Leaving the lamp where it sat on the table by his cot, he limped stiffly over to Jazz.

"Don't move," he mumbled as he pulled his hunting knife free.

Jazz felt the cold hardness of the steel press against her left ankle and slide down to where the zip tie was rubbing the skin raw. There was pressure, a back-and-forth tugging, and suddenly her left ankle was free! She jerked it in towards her bum. Wanted to wave it around.

"Stop it," Stoker said. "Hold still or I can't free the other one."

Her other one. Both feet. She dropped her left foot and straightened the leg. Stoker slid the knife under the zip tie holding her right foot and began the back and forth tugging that she knew was the knife sawing through the zip tie.

And then the right ankle was free too.

She took a breath and kicked hard at him, hoping for his testicles.

Her feet hit empty air. And came down hard off the side of the cot, half-twisting her off the edge so the metal frame cut into her thigh. "Agh!" Her lower back felt wrenched out of place. Strained muscles. Probably as much from having been strapped down to the goddamned cot for days as anything. "Damn it!"

She swung her lower half back onto the cot and looked to see Stoker standing a couple feet back from the cot, watching with a tiny smile. Because he'd known what she'd do. Anticipated it. Stepped back. And she'd gone and done exactly what he'd thought she would.

Double damn it.

"I can just let you pee your bed," he said now. "Or are you lying about needing to pee? You are due."

Her focus shot back down her body and she realized her faked need was actually real.

"I need to pee."

"Okay," Stoker said. "I'm going to free your wrists but hold onto one of them. You hit me or anything else and I'll hold both. Sorry, but we can't afford to have you damage anything here. It's all we've got."

Jazz thought about it, calculated her chances of over-powering him, spent a full beat amazed that she was actually thinking like that, of striking back, of actually fighting a man who was dominating her. She thought Aaron had beaten that all out of her, but apparently not. Her earlier thoughts had been right—she had a wild animal inside her like her mother had said, and it was slowly coming back to life.

But not enough. And not in this body of hers that had been strapped down for three days with almost no food and water. Quite putting aside the fact that Stoker outweighed her by probably fifty pounds, all muscle. And had a knife. Yeah.

She nodded at Stoker and he stepped back to her cot, around the top of it so there was even less chance she could strike him if she couldn't help herself.

Left wrist free. Ahh. Oh God, she hadn't realized how much pain she'd been in.

Right wrist free. Also amazing.

She went to shake her hands out only to have Stoker clamp his fingers around her right wrist, completely enveloping it. She whimpered and he held her a little less tightly.

"Come on," he said, and pulled her to a sitting position, her feet now planted on the floor. "Can you stand?"

She nodded and he wrapped an arm around her back, helping her rise up.

"Ooh. Light headed."

"Take your time."

But it wasn't passing quickly enough and she sagged into Stoker's chest. His bare chest. Hairy. Warm. She breathed into it. Comforted by his smell and the feel of his arm around her. Hating that response in her.

"You smell bad," she said. "You stink." She still felt like she might collapse. "What's with the necklace. What do you got hanging on it?"

"Nothing. Come on. Let's walk."

With one of his arms supporting her around her back and the other hand still securely holding her right wrist, he guided her between the rows of shelves and to the far end of the second row of shelves nearer the side of the room where Stoker's cot was. Jazz almost cried when she saw the bulky white plastic toilet rising up from the concrete with what looked like a pull out container on the bottom front and a large bucket of dry dirt—peat moss?—to one side.

"Composting toilet," Stoker said. "Not perfect because the ventilation shaft melted up top, I think. But it'll do for us for the time we're here. Go ahead. Use no more than two or three squares of tissue when you're done. One squirt of hand sanitizer."

So saying, he turned his head away from her but didn't release her wrist.

Jazz froze for a moment, then fumbled down her panties with her left hand, took a moment to examine her vagina to see if there was bruising from a rape while she'd been unconscious, but couldn't see anything. Of course, the lantern light only half-reached this space and everything was half in shadow, but she was pretty sure, as she touched herself, that she hadn't been violated by Stoker yet. At least not roughly. Her time with Aaron had left her far too familiar with what that felt like. So...

She turned and mounted the toilet. She peed, found the squares of tissue to dry herself, and dropped it into the space below her without looking at what was down there. She hopped off and pulled up her panties again. Found the hand sanitizer and felt a ridiculous surge of pleasure at the cold feel and sharp smell of alcohol on her fingers.

"Done."

Stoker turned back towards her, then reached past to scoop some of the dirt from the bucket into the toilet. He closed the lid.

"Peat moss and hemp," he said. "You can use dry grass clippings, coconut grass, other stuff."

She stared at him. "If this is a game, it's the sickest one I've ever read about."

"A game? Why of course it is. I'm manipulating you, creating this whole scenario, composting toilet and all, so you'll fall in love with me because that's so much more satisfying than just raping you."

*Raping.* The brutality of how he said it made her insides freeze. And he must have seen it because he shook his head and his free hand started tapping its fingers against his leg.

"Joking, Ms. Kazmi. Jesus. Reminder to self: Do not try

to joke with a concussed paranoid, or any time after one a.m."

He shook it off and tugged her out from behind the supply shelves, walked her back to her cot and made her lie down.

"Please, do you have to...?"

He zip-tied her right wrist to the side rail of the cot without answering. Then her left. Then her feet, one after the other, grabbing them hard when she started to squirm. When he was done, he looked long and hard at her face without meeting her eyes, then walked back to his own cot.

She called after him: "Can you leave the light on?"

He shook his head. "Like everything else, it's rationed to last us for two weeks. Besides, we both need our sleep. Light's the only thing that keeps up the circadian rhythms."

"I'm going to scream if you put it out. I'm afraid of what will come for me in the dark." Truth. A truth she hadn't really been aware of until she said, but truth nonetheless.

"Tough."

He glared at her then dialed off the lamp until the mantle sputtered, went out. Total blackness.

Jazz heard her breaths—one, two...

She screamed.

Stopped.

And again she heard just her own breathing.

Stoker's watch ticking.

CHAPTER 13

MORNING.

When Jazz was a little girl, it meant the sun beaming in through her window and hearing her father puttering about in the kitchen downstairs. Because breakfast was his meal. He was a short, hearty man who worked as a night watchman for the railways but was always home by six a.m. and loved making breakfast for his wife and daughter.

Always he boiled up water for the orange pekoe tea he'd adopted in England before emigrating to America. It was the perfect complement for bread, spread with feta or cream cheese, and a dollop of jam and maybe mint or basil leaves on top.

Always.

And Jazz's mother would bring Jazz from her room to the kitchen where they would all hug one another, say a Muslim du'a and a Christian grace, then eat with gusto. Jazz's father would tell of his night. Jazz would recount any dreams she remembered. Jazz's mother would be the perfect audience, oohing and ahing at all the right moments.

Even after Jazz's father got sick, even after he could no

longer work, there had always been the morning tea and bread and cheese.

Those were real mornings. Real breakfasts.

Unlike the first conscious one she spent with Stoker in the basement that gave her store-bought granola with milk made from milk powder and water. Then the lunch of unleavened bread with peanut butter and apple slices.

Stoker's food was served with hidden malice and disguised intentions. It did not nourish the soul or body.

CHAPTER 14

For dinnertime, Stoker turned the lantern light higher than before, like he wanted to artificially cheer Jazz up with his extravagance. It mostly highlighted the starkness of the concrete walls and battered shelves. The more she could see of the basement, the more it closed in on her.

Still, just as Stoker had done for breakfast and lunch, he freed Jazz's wrists so she could sit up on her cot and feed herself. And when he went back to his small gas camp stove, Jazz felt herself start salivating. Because just being actually awake for an entire day had brought back her appetite. The smell of scrambled eggs and beef jerky were driving her wild.

Stoker walked over with a plate of the eggs and jerky and set it down in front of her. She was about to scoop it up with her fingers when Stoker held up his hand.

"As with the cereal this morning...a spork!"

He handed it to her. Plastic. A spoon with short tines along the top. She took it wordlessly, lifted the plate of food with her other hand, and forced herself to eat slowly. To inhale the buttery rich smell of the eggs, savor the salty, bloody taste of the jerky, roll the eggs and bits of dried flesh in her mouth. Swallow. Sustenance. Living the now was one of the few things that had helped her survive Aaron.

Live the now. Focus on what is good. Close your eyes if you have to in order to shut out the rest.

"You realize it's been almost eight hours without a word," Stoker said.

She opened her eyes and looked at him. He'd finished his own food and pulled over the chair to within a couple feet of her. He sat watching her like she was some kind of circus act.

"It's impressive," he said. "I'm guessing it's the cocaine withdrawal or you're letting me think over my sins, consider what I'm doing here. Think how much you resemble my daughter and how cruel it is to keep you strapped to your cot. Any of those?"

Jazz swallowed her last bite of eggs and stared at Stoker for a good half-minute before saying, "I'm mostly thinking you're not beating me. And you haven't raped me. Yet."

Stoker nodded. "Clever. Good observations."

"But I'm still tied up."

"I explained that."

Jazz nodded at the shelves. "Camp gear. Water. Food. Two cots. Explain those."

"I like how you're stronger when you turn your situation into an intellectual challenge. Good for you. Does it signal a willingness to be rational and actually consider the evidence?"

"Answer the question."

Stoker smiled. "Earthquake preparedness. We live along one of the worst fault lines in the world. You have to be able to take care of yourself."

"Mr. Boy Scout."

"Pretty much." He looked away from her and his face clouded. "And I was trying to set a good example for Aaron and Elizabeth."

"An example."

"It's one of those things you do as a parent."

"Do tell."

But his focus had gone somewhere else, and for a moment she actually believed his soul was tortured. Like maybe he had lost something. His innocence? His connection with his children? But how could a kidnapping psychopath, who deceived everyone in his life about what he did, feel anything about anyone?

Finally his head snapped up. "You lost your parents, Aaron said. Your dad a while back. Your mother a couple months ago. How?"

*No. You don't get that.* "Why didn't anyone hear me scream?"

Stoker raised his eyebrows. "There's...no one to hear it."

"Right. That what you meant."

"What?"

"When you said we'd get to that later. You sealed up the door so no one would hear me scream."

"I sealed up the door so...?"

He shook his head sadly and stood up. After taking Jazz's plate and spork from her, he walked to the small plastic tub of water he'd set up beside the basement floor drain. He squatted there and rinsed and cleaned them, along with his own, which had been soaking. When he was done, he poured the gray water into the drain.

"Three days I was out," Jazz said to recapture his attention.

"Mostly."

"Did I pee or poop during that time?"

"Yes. And yes, I cleaned you up. I also used some improvised diapers so your cot stayed clean."

Jazz felt herself blushing hot. "That's lovely. That's just... Did it turn you on somehow? Are you one of those guys who gets off on really kinky shit?"

Stoker rose with the dishes, shook the water off them, and walked to the middle storage shelf near his cot. He put away the dishes, then went back to his box of zip ties took out two more.

No. *No.* Jazz felt her wrists already burning in anticipation.

"You know," he said as he walked back to her, "there may well have been a time when I imagined having sex with you. I'm not dead. And you can be...attractive. There may also come a time when I want to hold you close in much the same way you clung to Aaron when you lost all the people you loved. But trust me when I say..." He motioned for her to lie down and put her wrists in position.

No. "I didn't cling to Aaron."

"What?"

"I just needed his money. When my mom died, she had no insurance. I was broke. I was scared. Aaron found out and offered me a place to live."

The money part was true. The part about not clinging was a lie to hurt Stoker now. To make him think his son had been used by her, not clung to in the desperate existential need she'd felt when her mother, the last remaining pillar of her emotional life, had been struck by a car and died in hospital less than a day later. "Scared" hadn't been even the half of it. Despite her academic achievements, the part-time jobs she'd held to help her mother with their rent, even the boys who'd chased her, her mother's death had wrecked her. Being suddenly alone in the world had made her feel helpless. Less than worthless. She'd dropped into a black hole so deep that she'd considered ending it all.

Then Aaron had offered her a hand up, drugs to stop the suicidal thoughts and get her going again. When he finally offered her a place to stay as well, it was like a choice between drowning on her own or climbing onto a shiny boat.

The beatings and emotional abuse started later.

"I thought..." Stoker said now.

"He figured if he was supporting me, he could do pretty much anything he wanted with me." Which seemed reasonable for so long. Too long. "Did you teach him that, Professor? Cause it's what you're doing now, isn't it?"

Stoker frowned, tugging the zip ties back and forth between his fingers. "I'm...not doing anything with you but keeping us both safe."

"Aaron used to hit me and choke me. You just strap me down."

Stoker's face had gone red, the upset real. "He... That doesn't fit the boy I..."

"But these do?" She jerked her feet back and forth against their painful plastic bands so that the entire cot swayed and creaked.

"You know what those are, Ms. Kazmi? And these?" He held up the zip ties he planned to tie down her wrists with. "They're metaphors. You have the power to take them off. Just like you always had the power to get away from my son. But the stories you run in your head about who you are, the power you do or don't have, where you belong in the world, they're like little plastic zip ties. They obviously kept you zipped into Aaron's apartment. Now they're keeping you zipped to that cot."

Jazz swallowed back the bile that rose in her throat and

said, "So I can just tell myself a new story and they fall away?"

"No. You don't just tell yourself a story, Ms. Kazmi. You open your eyes and ears and brain and truly experience the story you're in."

"Right. Tied to a cot, waiting for you stop playing and start hurting me."

He grimaced. "At some point I'm going to tell you my story. My history. What I lost *before* all of this. Before you. And you will understand what a mind-numbingly stupid thing it was that you just said. You'll see where this is going and how it all has to end."

"Tell me now.

He stared at her like he wanted to rip her face off. "You don't know how to listen yet."

"Fuck you."

"And you. I can't believe I once thought you were a good student. Now lie down, put your wrists to the side of the cot. It's almost bedtime again."

No no no no no. "And if I don't?"

"You really want to find out? I'm game. Go ahead and struggle."

Heart beating wildly, Jazz held his stare until she felt her wild animal resolve crumble inside her like so much wet cardboard. She lay back and placed her wrists to the sides of the cot just below her waist level.

Stoker put a zip tie around each and zipped them closed.

Cursing pathetically at herself in her head, she turned her face from him. Heard him pull his chair back to the table near his cot. The dull static of the radio turned up louder and fizzed in and out as Stoker obviously was seeking for a message across the airwave bands.

No joy. Nothing but static.

The light went darker in the room. Stoker was either saving gas or trying to signal it was almost night time. Sleep time.

And despite Jazz's disgust over how the minute she'd started talking with him this evening, she'd stepped right into every emotional trap he'd set for her, she found her body shutting down and sleep rolling over her in an unstoppable wave.

He was smarter, stronger, in control. There was no way Jazz could... No way she could... Couldn't...

"Give me answers," she ordered her brain.

Her eyes closed.

AGAIN THERE WAS no lamp burning, but this time a diffuse light from somewhere lit both her cot and Stoker's cot across the floor from her.

Aaron stood beside Stoker's cot, looking down at his sleeping father.

"What a load of bullshit," Aaron said.

"What is?" Jazz said.

Aaron didn't acknowledge her, but a snort from the wall near the stairs revealed Elizabeth standing there. "He is," Elizabeth said. "My brother the psychopath."

Aaron shook his head without taking his eyes off his father. "Sociopath, maybe. Because I was raised by this sonofabitch."

Jazz looked to the wall of shelves now and saw Lindsay standing halfway between Jazz's cot and Stoker's. "I don't know whether to be offended or relieved by that statement. I mean, I was there, wasn't I, dear?"

"Telling us how to think," Aaron shot back. "Playing games with our feelings."

"Maybe I wasn't," Lindsay said.

Elizabeth broke in. "He wanted to educate us! To make us better people!"

Lindsay laughed at that. At poor, stupidly naïve, blind Elizabeth.

"He wanted to control us," Aaron said. "Because the strong control the weak always. Remember that."

"But what does he want now?" Jazz asked.

"He already told you, babe."

A thumping started somewhere. Jazz craned her head to look around but couldn't pinpoint where it was coming from.

"What's that?" she said.

Aaron snickered. "Morning wants in. Somebody wants you to wake up. Maybe you."

More thumping. From the door? From the door at the top of the stairs? Jazz heard a cracking sound. A muffled curse.

"But I need to know what he wants from me!" she cried. "How do I prepare if I don't know what he wants!"

One more loud thump sounded form the direction of the stairs and suddenly Santino wandered out of the gap between the shelves and stood beside Lindsay.

He looked around and grinned. "Hey, I just took a shit. You smell it?"

"I smell it," Elizabeth said.

"Lord, yes," said Lindsay.

"I smell it," Aaron said.

And Jazz cried out, "I don't! I don't! I don't! I don't!"

With each cry, one of her imaginary guests vanished. Then the light popped into blackness and...

CHAPTER 16

Jazz woke to see the lantern lit over on the table and Stoker sitting on the chair right beside her cot. His face dripped sweat as he hunched forward towards her. His fingers held his little black book and a pen. His eyes were drinking her in with an intensity she couldn't read.

"What time is it?" she asked.

"You really are beautiful."

"The time?"

His eyes raked over her body and returned to her face. "Even sweaty, dirty, bruised. Your lips, chapped as they are, curve with such...sensuality."

It was like being raped by his eyes. And by the fact he didn't even seem to hear her. Didn't acknowledge she was awake, could see him, could think and feel. Like she was the nothing she'd been right after her mother died. Then again a nothing after Aaron began to beat and control her. A nothing. A no one. Without even drugs to hide from the horror of that.

Heat and tears welled up and squeezed out of her eyes.

Stoker craned his neck in fascination at the sight.

"It's eight fifteen," he said. "A.M."

Jazz swallowed. "I need to use the toilet."

"All right."

He whipped out his hunting knife and cut all her zip ties so quickly she barely had time to react to the pain of it. He hauled her to her feet and walked her back to the gap Santino had come out of in her dreams. Stoker gave her a little shove in. As she almost banged into the plastic toilet, she turned to see Stoker was blocking the exit, but with his back turned.

"Ration the tissue," he said. "When you're done, one scoop each of the peat moss and hemp."

Jazz rubbed her wrists, working some circulating back into them. She rotated her feet. Finally she tugged down her panties and climbed up on the toilet seat without looking in.

And had a bizarre bout of shyness.

"Don't listen!" she said.

No response. Dead silence, in fact, other than the distant hiss of the gas lantern, Stoker shifting about, Jazz's own labored breathing, then...

Tinkling. Farts. An involuntary grunt as she passed a thick stool that plopped onto what sounded like a mound of dirt.

Lovely.

When she was done, she stood, used four tissue squares, then scooped in the peat moss and hemp. All without looking or breathing. Squirt of hand sanitizer.

She reemerged, pushing out past him, and his hand gripped her left arm, guiding her back to her cot. He made her sit and zip-tied her ankles to the cot rails, leaving her wrists free so she could sit up.

"It sounded satisfying," he said.

Then he stood and walked back to the food shelves near

his cot. He pulled out oats, dried apples, and nuts from their respective resealable containers, put them in his small cooking pot, poured in some water, and fired up the small cooking stove he pulled off the bottom shelf to sit on the floor near Stoker's cot.

"You recall what you told me in class the day you and Aaron came over?" he said like he was just making conversation.

"No," Jazz said. "Okay, maybe. That China was too scared of the US to sign a treaty?"

"What I'm remembering," Stoker said as he stirred in the oats, fruit, and nuts, "is your comment about Ma Yang cozying up to Putin to distract him so China could bomb the US."

"I was being a smartass."

Stoker nodded, focusing on his cookpot. Stirring slowly. "Of course you were. Quoting Sun Tzu: All warfare is based on deception. Why haven't you tried that with me?"

"Tried..."

"Deceiving me. I'm obviously your enemy, so why haven't you tried cozying up to me so I'll free you from your bondage?"

What the hell? Was this an invitation or a challenge? A way out? Jazz looked carefully at Stoker, but the man was just calmly making their porridge. Breakfast. Like he could have been her father making their breakfast. Except her father had never hit her over the head, strapped her to a cot, and carried on conversations about once wanting to have sex with her, or being the enemy and inviting her to "cozy up" to him.

But what Jazz kept coming back to was the implicit promise that she could win her freedom if she played this right.

"How am I supposed to cozy up to you when I'm tied up?" she said.

He stopped stirring for a moment and looked directly at her. "I guess you're going to have to convince me to untie you."

"How do I do that?"

He shook his head and went to the shelves for the skim milk powder. Mixed up maybe a cup-and-a-half's worth as he said, "Really, Ms. Kazmi? You want me to just give you the answer sheet? At least *try* to think it through. You were taking a fourth year political science course with me that covered negotiations. Well this is Negotiations 101. You have something you want. The other party, me, has something I want. Is it a zero-sum game?"

"Um...no. Zero-sum means anything party A wins is subtracted from what party B wins, bickering over a finite, singular resource. It's not that."

"Because..."

"Me getting what I want doesn't mean you can't get what you want."

"So it can be win win," Stoker said, stirring the porridge again. "Spell it out."

"I want to be released from this cot."

"Okay. And me?"

"You want to...have sex with me?"

Stoker stopped stirring the porridge and dropped his head as if profoundly disappointed. Then he shook it off, spooned the porridge into two bowls, added milk to each, stuck a spork into each, and brought them both over to Jazz's cot. He sat in his chair and handed Jazz's bowl to her.

It was still steaming, even with the milk. Jazz stirred it, took a small spoonful and blew on it.

"You have a remarkably one-track brain," Stoker said as

she nibbled on the spoonful and blew some more. Stoker himself seemed content to stir in his milk and let it cool before eating.

Jazz risked the entire spoonful. It burned the top of her mouth but she didn't care. She was hungry and it was a distraction. Stoker was literally a foot away from her. She could smell him. She could almost feel his aura, electricity, whatever. The *presence* of him. In her personal space, over which she apparently had no control anymore.

"Two tracks, if you include food, I suppose," he said. "I keep forgetting how much difficulty you have separating your internal fictions from reality. Unless it really is para-noia from the bump on your head or drug withdrawal. Or maybe extreme narcissism."

He looked at her like he was expecting a response. She took another spoonful and blew on it. Blew some more.

"Try again, Ms. Kazmi. What do I want from you?"

She lowered her spoon again, finally understanding the game. "You want...me to believe you."

"Better! But totally intangible. What would that entail?"

"Um...saying it? No, saying *why* I believe you."

"And?"

Her brain raced over everything he'd said earlier—his bullshit, his thinly disguised (in retrospect) requirements for her to be free of the cot. "Promise to remain calm?"

"Getting there."

"I show you I can *be* calm and civilized. That I will rationally consider the evidence and then, if I find it credi-ble, help you, help us, survive."

"Good!" he said like he'd always done in class when someone had finally fed back to him what he thought was an extremely obvious truth about how the bigger world worked. "And what will you do to help us survive?"

"You mean..." Was it all back to sex after all?

He grimaced. "No. I don't mean that. I mean what survival skills do you possess? Do you know how to cook? Operate the radio? Inventory supplies? Check for radiation leaks?"

"You have a Geiger counter?"

"You're listening. Good. No. My earthquake preparedness didn't contemplate radiation. The other skills?"

"I can learn. I will learn."

"Because..."

Asking why she wanted to learn? She studied his face. No, asking why she might go along with this. In the bigger context, why he could believe that she was actually honest in actually trying to believe all his bullshit when she'd already called him on it over and over.

"Mostly because of the heat," she said at last. "The forecast when Aaron and I came for dinner was a week of cold and rain. Now, it's possible we had a heat wave or something, but the heat in here is just one of a lot of things that fit your explanations of what happened better than mine."

"Like?" She could hear the excitement in his voice. He was practically creaming his dress pants.

"Your clothes. You staying locked down here with me in the same clothes you wore three days ago. Eating crappy rations. Sleeping on a cot. That doesn't make sense if you just wanted sex with me. You could leave and come back. You could tempt me with good food or drugs. You could just rape me. You'd have to be totally obsessed and a pretty fucking good actor to do all this just so I'd *choose* to sleep with you. Occam's razor, right?"

"Exactly."

Stoker's porridge had cooled and now he ate, as if the discussion they'd just had made everything right with the world and he could finally enjoy a simple breakfast.

Jazz ate her porridge too, though it mostly tasted like sawdust on her tongue. Her brain was racing too hard, trying to get ahead of Stoker. See where this was going. How could she use what he'd just exposed of himself and his feelings to get herself free? Not only free of her zip ties, but free of Stoker. And...what if she couldn't get free of him? What happened then?

Stoker finished his bowl and licked it clean, encouraging her to do the same with hers. Different rules of the table when you had limited rations. No waste permitted.

He reached for her bowl and she gave it up.

"One more thing?" she said.

"Yes?"

"Do we have any electricity down here? No. Of course not. The gas lantern. The crank radio. What about my cell phone or yours? Do either of them have any power left?"

"You're thinking. Good."

Stoker rose with the bowls and sporks and took them back to the cleaning area. He rinsed and cleaned them down by the floor drain, then put them away and went for Jazz's purse, now hidden behind some items on an upper shelf.

He opened the purse and pulled out her cracked phone. Tried turning it on. Nothing.

He went to the table and pulled out his own cell phone from behind the radio. He turned it on and walked it over to show her.

"Low battery. No signal," he said. "And yes, I've made calls from this basement before. AT&T 4G. Just put a new ring tone on the day of the big bomb."

He flipped through the settings menu and found the ringtones, played the new one, a classical piece Jazz didn't recognize, then powered off the phone again.

"I turn it on briefly every few days just to check," he said. "Just in case."

"In case emergency crews come in and fix the cell tower?"

"I guess."

"Wouldn't it make more sense to preserve the battery for when we go out? Stick to the radio for now?"

Stoker stared at her, then his face split in a huge smile. "Actually...yes. That's the sort of obvious thing you get when you have someone else to talk to."

"Meaning someone who's not tied up and denying the reality of what's happened. Like I've been."

He looked ready to cry. "Yes."

"But like I'm not now."

"All warfare is deception."

"You keep asking me to trust you," Jazz said. "Take a chance the other way."

CHAPTER 17

Stoker stared at her a moment, then wandered his phone back to its place by the radio. After setting it down, he walked back to the foot-end of Jazz's cot, pulled out his hunting knife, and cut her ankles free.

She leaned down and rubbed them as he watched her. Then she swung them off the bed and stood, fighting less dizzy weakness than she had the last few times. She stretched out her arms, stomped her bare feet a few times on the cement floor, and hugged herself.

"My shoes?" she said.

"They're under your cot."

"Ha!" Jazz turned and bent down, saw the high heels she'd been wearing, and left them there. When she stood up, she saw that Stoker was still watching her closely.

"Can I walk around?" she asked.

He nodded. "Just don't touch anything unless you ask first because... Never mind. Yes. Walk."

So she did, feeling like a toddler under the watchful eye of father Stoker making sure she doesn't destroy the glass figurines.

She wandered back behind the first row of shelving to check out the second row of supplies, and the random household junk—paint cans, a broken bicycle, Christmas ornaments—behind that. What really astounded her was how little she could smell the composting toilet even back here. It couldn't vent to the outside, so how...?

The question dropped away as Stoker's head appeared at the end of the row, watching her.

She nodded and skipped back into the open area with the cots.

"Can I go up the stairs and check the door?" she asked.

Directly behind her, he said, "Sure," and she jumped.

She climbed the stairs with Stoker behind her. At the top, she considered whether this could have been the one she remembered coming through four days ago. It was covered with what looked like fiberglass batting and plastic. Even the doorknob and hinges were covered over, the former identifiable only by the extra bump at her hip level where she expected it to be. The 2x4's Jazz had seen Stoker carrying up the stairs the day before rested horizontally, one across the top half of the door, one across the bottom, held tightly in by brackets screwed on either side of the door itself, compressing the plastic and fiberglass batting tight under them, keeping the door from swinging open intwards.

Jazz looked back at Stoker. "Why the security bars?"

He began drumming his fingers against his leg. "Something, flying debris, hit the door a couple days ago. I was worried it was going to crash right through it."

"So how do we get out? When it's time."

"We lift out the bars, cut off the cover, and open the door."

Jazz had a sudden flash of what Stoker had looked like

with his shirt off. The necklace with something hanging from it.

"Is that what's on your necklace?" she said. "The key to the door?"

"It's a basement door. It doesn't lock from inside."

"So what's—?"

Stoker turned from her abruptly and headed back down the stairs, calling back, "Do you want to learn how to use the radio?"

Jazz nodded to herself. "Sure."

Before she followed him down, though, she ran her hand around the outside of the door, feeling how secure the tape was that secured the covering. She put her ear it, as well, but heard almost nothing. Maybe a very dull roar. An engine sound? Wind? Where *was* this basement they were trapped in?

"You coming down?" Stoker called.

"Coming!"

She hurried down the steps but stopped at the bottom when she spotted the baseball bat leaning against a shelf. Just like that. Out in the open.

She picked it up and examined it closely, reading the printing on it, looking for dents or her own blood and hair. Saw Stoker watching her.

"Coast Little League Tigers," she said.

She walked with it in her hands, swinging it back and forth, looking at Stoker as she did, sizing up how fast and hard she'd have to swing to hit his head.

Stoker rested his hand on his knife top. "Choices every second, aren't there."

"I played slow pitch as a kid," Jazz said. "I was good."

"Kept your eye on the ball."

"Swung at just the right time."

"And if you hit it just right and ran," Stoker said, "where'd you go? First base? Second? Or all the way back to where you started?"

Jazz swung the bat again. "Maybe home for milk and cookies."

"Maybe."

Jazz had reached her cot. She casually leaned down and put the bat on the floor just under the door side of the cot before straightening and smiling at Stoker. "I was never *that* good."

Then she walked deliberately to him and sat in the chair in front of the table. Reached out to run her fingers over the turn-crank-powered radio. Behind her, the electricity that was Stoker leaned close over her, probably drinking her in. Maybe trying to look down the top of her dress.

Stoker reached past her and turned the crank for about ten seconds to power it up. He pointed at a switch.

"On. Off."

She flipped it on and the lights lit up.

"Turn the dial.

She did, getting the familiar buzz of static with the occasional blip.

"There's probably still too much electromagnetic interference from the blast," Stoker said. "Or there's no one transmitting near enough. But at some point FEMA, someone, will broadcast."

"And we'll hear it down here?"

He put his two hands on her shoulders for a second, seemed to realize the threat it could be taken for and removed them. It made her giddy for a second that her reaction was so important to him. That at this moment, freed of her cot, she held some measure of power.

"We're not buried in so much rubble that we can't breathe," he answered her question. "So yes. We'll hear it down here."

"And talk back to whoever?"

"In theory."

"And your black book? Are those notes about—?"

She'd reached for it as she asked, but he snatched it away. "Private."

"What about your necklace? Your history? Are you ever going to share those? For real?"

He leaned tiredly on the table to look at her. "Give it time, Ms. Kazmi. You're no longer strapped to your cot. That's something, isn't it?"

"Are they things you're embarrassed about? Scared how I'll react? Come on, just..."

Jazz reached for the necklace beneath his shirt, but her touch sent him scrambling backwards, sputtering.

"Jesus Christ, I said not to touch anything! That includes me, okay?"

"I just..."

Stoker bared his teeth at her. "You just want whatever's on your mind. Whatever will make *you* feel good or safe or vindicated, smart. You put on an act of being open and reasonable, but you're neither of those. You're shallow and scared and reptilian. Looking for how to gain an advantage, how to hoodwink or physically overcome me so that you can prove to yourself I'm the devil and you've once again been kidnapped and abused. A victim! Go ahead and deny it."

"It's not true."

"Ha. And now you see? I don't believe you. Like you don't believe me."

He smiled in triumph when he said it but she could see the sadness leaking out. She still had the power here. She wasn't sure why, but she could feel it like a fine skein of molasses in the air, something connecting her and Stoker so that his every twitch signaled something to her. So she wasn't sure if he was playing her or she, him.

But when he spoke again, it told her that at least this time she was right. She had control.

"What will it take for you to believe me, Ms. Kazmi? Jasmine. Jazz. What will it take?"

She tugged her invisible string. "You know what it will take."

"What? I truly don't."

And with all her invisible strength—"Let me see outside."

Stoker frowned. "What?"

"Outside. Open the door and let me see the post-apocalyptic landscape you say is out there." *Come on. Come on.*

He looked wonderingly at her. "Open the door...?"

CHAPTER 18

STOKER HAD PULLED his hunting knife from his belt sheath unconsciously and started fondling it. Was that to cut away the door covering or to cut Jazz for pushing too hard? Jazz swallowed dryly and decided to pull every invisible string he could feel, even as they slipped from her grasp.

"It's one simple thing," she said. "Come on. If it's as you say—fires burning, radiation everywhere—then I'll get burned a bit, maybe get a dose of it. Just a second or two."

He smiled again—he did that so often—but this time it hid something deep and dark and terrifying. What she imagined Aaron might become with another twenty years of growing in power and deceit. "And if you see we're in a run-down neighborhood at the edge of town that clearly hasn't been destroyed by nuclear bombs or anything else..."

She tried to swallow and couldn't. He was in her head, playing *her*. But to what end? To make her back down? Withdraw her request? Go along with his game rather than face what happened when the make-believe ended?

"Then," she said, her voice cracking, "we'll know where we stand, won't we?"

"Yes we will."

He held her gaze, looking into her, every part of her, before he turned and walked to an upper shelf near her cot. He came away from it with a large roll of duct tape, went back to the table for the lantern, and walked to the bottom of the stairs. He put down the lantern there and turned and gestured for Jazz to join him.

She wiped her mouth and walked to him.

"You first," he said.

So she climbed, even knowing it was so he could watch her ass as she did. Though if he'd already cleaned her and done whatever to her when she'd been unconscious, why should he care?

And she answered herself: the power, of course. Stripping an unconscious young woman had none of the thrill of controlling a conscious one. And the sex had to be part of that, too. Like a lion wanting live prey. It was the struggle and kill that turned Stoker on. That was the game.

Jazz shuddered as the rightness of that revelation clicked into place. And just as quickly, she began processing deep in her mind how she could use this understanding to beat him. Because she was never going back to being the nothing Aaron made her into. Never.

She'd reached the top of the stairs and Stoker pushed her to the right side so he could crowd up on the step with her, face to face, breathing hard, him by the covered-lump where the doorknob was.

"I'm going to lift out the security bars," he said, "then cut the tape along this edge and just enough of the top and bottom to pull open the door a crack."

Jazz nodded. "Enough to look out but not run out, right?"

"To minimize the damage."

"And keep me under control."

Stoker didn't react to her last comment. He just held her eyes, then put the duct tape down on the stair below. Jazz stepped down a couple steps to give him room as he pulled out his knife and did what he said he would. Careful not to rip the insulation, he cut the line of duct tape that held it down to the floor. Sliced it approximately three feet across, using precise, sure movements that showed the tip of the knife was as sharp as any box cutter. Then he did the left-side tape, top to bottom. Finally the top, three feet across like the bottom.

The edges of the insulation popped a bit, exposing the pink fiberglass under the backing paper, but they didn't fall from the door like Jazz had expected they would. Double-sided tape or something?

She smelled dust and imagined tiny glass particles floating through the air and into her nose, something her father had warned her about once when adding more insulation to the ceiling of their rented house. It filled Jazz with a vague panic, which she knew was beyond silly. She was already facing Stoker's possible intent to rape and kill her or the fact World War Three had begun. She could handle fiberglass dust.

But what the panic was really about, she realized, was her indecision over what she was going to do next. When she opened that door, even a small crack and saw not devastation but some field or suburb just out of town, what was she going to do? Rip the door back and run? Stoker would catch her.

What if she screamed for help as she ran?

He'd probably planned for that, too. Either they were too far from any neighbors for screams to be heard, or Stoker wouldn't give her the chance. A blow to the head. An arm around the waist. Her mind flashed back to seeing him without his shirt. Muscular in an almost brutal way. Beyond all the learning and sophisticated speech, Scott Stoker was as much a wild beast underneath as Jazz. And stronger. More experienced in bringing down his prey.

While her brain ran the scenarios, Stoker had slid his hand in behind the insulation to find and test the doorknob. Now he pulled it out, re-sheathed his knife, and turned to Jazz, looking down on her with his face serious.

"So here's the deal," he said. "You turn the knob. You open it no more than a few inches. You see what there is to see. You shut it quickly."

Jazz's brain raced. "Fifteen seconds? Ten?"

"Just enough so you know the truth."

The *truth*. And the truth shall set you free?

"Wait," he said when she hesitated.

"What?"

"Stay right there."

Then he trotted down the stairs and there was just her and the door. The unlocked door. If she went through it right now, she'd have a head start. Not much. But a few seconds. And she'd always been a good runner, so even in her hungry, muscle-atrophied state, she could—

"Got 'em!"

Jazz looked back down the stairs to see Stoker running up them again, carrying a pair of sunglasses and slipping something into his pants pocket. Her heart pounded, and she had rushes of ice through her veins like the fire of adrenaline had flooded in then flooded away when she'd waited too long to act. Stupid girl. Not a beast but a scared cow.

He held out the sunglasses. "Might want to put these on. Protect your eyes."

She looked at them and shook her head. He shrugged

and stuck them into his pocket. Then he stepped right up behind her on the top step. She could feel his heat, his tangible excitement.

"Any time," he said.

Swallowing dryly, Jazz slid her left hand under the insulation as she'd seen Stoker do and found the doorknob. Turned it. Then she tugged gently. Harder. Finally grabbed the nob with both hands, turned it, and yanked it back with all her weight.

It scratched. Shuddered. She kept grunting and pulling.

Finally began to scrape open inwards. Six inches. Eighteen.

She stopped pulling and let go of the nob, exhausted. Spent.

She stepped up to the door opening, looked out, and saw...

CHAPTER 19

The world on fire.

The blasting heat of it hit Jazz before her eyes registered it, but she still had to *see* it to believe.

Whatever had blasted or rolled through here—and yes, in her mind's eye now she saw Stoker's nuclear blast and firestorm—had leveled maybe half the buildings and simply torn apart and set fire to the rest, leaving chimneys and random walls standing, most of a smokestack in the distance that had been part of a factory she hadn't know was there. Trees were jagged, black and smoking spikes of carbon. Cars were blown-out wrecks, some actively burning, spitting up spirals of thick, dark smoke. The asphalt itself was smoking and cracked, with huge potholes and missing swaths as if it had melted away at the firestorm's zenith, maybe been part of the gleeful burning that had obviously been going on for days.

Jazz wanted to stick her face out the door and look up and back to see what was left of the Stoker house, of Aaron and Elizabeth, Santino, Lindsay.

But she could hardly breathe. Her lungs were on fire.

Her face burned. Her legs were not obeying her orders to move.

Suddenly Stoker's hands were on the back of her dress, pulling her back from the door opening and pushing the door closed with the full weight of his body.

Grind. Click!

Jazz looked at him, his face serious, staring at her, then she stumbled down the stairs away from him. Away from the door.

Her brain wasn't functioning. No synapses firing. No reaction but shock.

She heard the scratching sounds of tape. The duct tape. Stoker re-taping the door covering that he'd cut to let her look out. Then the hollow clunking of the 2x4s as he lifted each and returned them to their brackets to keep the door closed.

Jazz still stood like a brainless machine at the bottom of the stairs when Stoker finally finished and came down to join her.

"It's better than it was a few days ago. The fires are dying. I should still put something on your face."

When she didn't answer—And why should she answer? Who was she and what did she have to do with a world that no longer made sense?—Stoker pulled from his pants pocket the jar he'd earlier taken from the shelves. He unscrewed the cap, dipped in two fingers and drew them out covered in clear goop. He began gently spreading it across Jazz's face. He covered her forehead, ran under the eyebrows, down the cheeks and nose, around her mouth, her chin.

"Just aloe vera," he said. "Should help a little. Hopefully prevent any permanent damage like mine. It's still going to hurt for a few days. You should drink something."

He left her for a few moments, then was back with a

cup of water that he held to her lips. She dutifully sipped at it until he lowered it.

He said, "It's a lot to take in, I know."

"They're all dead."

"Yes."

When she still didn't move, Stoker finally sighed and walked with the cup back to the table near his cot. She heard the scratch of the chair as he pulled it out and sat. Creak. Then the radio hissed and crackled as he cranked the handle for power and began dialing through the frequencies to find something other than static.

After a time, Jazz regained enough of herself to walk to her cot, sit on it, and fall over. She lay on her back, staring up at the sputtering shadows of the ceiling with unblinking eyes.

An hour passed.

Three?

Jazz was vaguely aware of Stoker offering her lunch. She didn't even look at him.

More time passed.

Stoker offered her dinner. Also ignored.

Because what did it matter?

Eventually, she subconsciously registered that Stoker shut off the radio he usually played with in the evening. There was a clanking as he put things away. Tidied up. Then the lantern light dropped.

"Good night," he called over.

The light went out, but...

CHAPTER 20

...THIS NIGHT JAZZ couldn't remember closing her eyes. Or dreaming.

Again, what was the point?

In the morning, she was awake, staring at the ceiling, when the scratch of Stoker's footsteps announced his approach. His face appeared between her and the ceiling. Standing. Looking down on her.

"Can I show you what we have for supplies?" he said. "Explain how I've calculated our rations? What I have planned for when we finally exit this shelter?"

He waited, his face hanging there above her, until some part of Jazz realized he wasn't going to move until she answered him. So she nodded vaguely.

Stoker smiled and took both of her hands. He pulled her up to sitting and swung her legs around and over the side of the cot.

Blinking, she held up her hand to stop him before he ducked in for a close hug to stand her up. Under her own power, she stood, blinked, looked around. It felt like everything should look different, but it didn't. It was her that was out of joint. Like she could no longer properly process her place in the world or what she was supposed to do.

"The shelves," Stoker prompted. He now held the gas lantern in his left hand.

She nodded and followed him to the shelves one row in. The ones to the right were mostly devoted to the composting toilet, he pointed out, but also had cleaning supplies and pest poisons. Though he had only encountered silverfish and beetles down here so far.

On the other side of the aisle, he held up the lantern so she could see the backup camp stove, a manual water pump, gas for the stove and lantern, blankets, and some boxes he didn't bother explaining.

He walked her back to the main part of the room and over to the shelves by his end of the cot. Here were the bags and boxes of rice and beans, oats, pudding cups. Cans of ham and fish. Canisters of water. And now, rather than just watch Stoker pick through this stuff to make meals, Jazz was treated to a lengthy monologue on food densities, nutrition, and storage practices. There was no cardboard or thin plastic because it got attacked by humidity, heat, and pests. Thick and airtight was the rule. Except for the freeze-dried foods, which, Stoker said, would have been the ideal for the longer-term survival the current situation could entail.

The water, similarly, was stored in two large food-grade, square, brown plastic canisters with spigots because the plastic in most smaller commercial containers would break down after two years (much less for plastic milk jugs) and you never knew how long your water would be sitting in the basement before a disaster called it into use.

Jazz was left amazed that they had any edible food and

potable water here at all, and wondered how a survivalist gene had crept into Stoker's otherwise elitist, academic, and possibly psychopathic makeup.

Beside the food were the main camp stove, dishes and cutlery. The next shelf held medical supplies, including the jar of aloe vera Stoker had used earlier and pill bottles which Stoker explained were antibiotics. There were also goggles, vodka, and toiletries.

A games shelf held cards, something Stoker said was a cribbage board, and a chess set.

The library shelf had both survival books and popular fiction.

Finally he took her back into the aisle between the shelves again, and led her to the third and final stand of shelves. It held rope, a saw, the duct tape, building tools. Random scrap wood and metal was stored behind it. Along with, presumably, more of the insulation batting that Stoker had dragged out to cover the basement door at the top of the stairs.

"First line of defense," Stoker said. "I call it my survival set."

"And that?" Jazz mumbled, after Stoker finished showing her how much random other junk was hidden behind the survival shelves.

"What?"

"The metal lockbox there."

"This?" Stoker lifted it off the top rear shelf, turned away from her as he moved the dials on the combination lock, and turned back to show her what was inside.

"It's..."

"A Glock .45," Stoker said. "With an extra ammunition clip."

"You know how to shoot it?"
"Oh yeah."
"Would you please use it to shoot me?"

CHAPTER 21

STOKER HAD CHUCKLED when she'd asked him to shoot her, assuming it was a joke.

Or just treating it as one.

*Had* it been a joke? Jazz didn't know.

She hadn't yet been able to pull herself out of the shock of finding the entire world she knew blown to pieces and burning. She now sat in the basement's second chair, on the far side of the radio table, listlessly eating the dried fruit and nuts Stoker had put in a bowl on the table for her.

He, meanwhile, sat in the other chair and fieldstripped the gun from the lockbox. He cleaned each piece with a cloth and carefully examined it for any unwanted bends, nicks, or bumps. Then he slammed it all back together and reinserted the clip he'd had in it.

"You know what I like about Glocks?" he said as he held it up in front of him with two hands and aimed it directly at Jazz's face.

Jazz stopped eating, feeling her heart kick back into gear. Almost. "What?"

"There's no external safety. You pull the trigger the whole way and blam!"

"Hunh."

He bent his elbows and brought the gun back to rest on the table between them. "So I've been reading and remembering and thinking through our situation almost since the bombs hit, and here's what I've come up with. We're about thirteen miles out from the city core. A modern nuclear weapon, if it was a ground blast, probably wouldn't have leveled everything this far out the way you saw outside.

"But an air blast would have. Near one hundred percent fatalities for anyone not in a concrete structure underground like we were. The advantage of an air blast for us is that the amount of fallout afterwards is a lot less, and determined mostly by which way the air is blowing.

"It looked to me out there like it's still blowing south. Meaning away from us. We'd up our chances of avoiding it even more if we walk east into the Cascade Mountains when we get out. That's also where there were probably fewer firestorms because of the uneven ground.

"We pack up enough food and water for two-to-four days hiking..."

He stopped and examined Jazz's face. And she wanted to be excited by what he was saying. Really. But she couldn't find a meaningful response.

"Are you following any of this?" Stoker asked.

Jazz licked the fruit sugar from her lips. "When do we leave?"

Stoker put the Glock back into the lockbox and closed the box. Locked it. Stood and, rather than walking down the middle aisle to the back shelf where it had been stored, he put it up above the stove and dishes near his cot. "When we leave," he said, "depends on how quickly the fires burn out.

On whether we hear signs of life on the radio before then. We're five days post blast. We'll probably need another five."

"When our supplies run out. You said we had ten days' rations."

"Three days, then. You saw outside. There's no point heading out into smoke and getting burned or trapped by wildfire."

"And no one's worried about us. No one waiting. No home to go to."

Stoker nodded. "Unfortunately accurate. So as long as we have our supplies, this is home. It's not luxury, but I've provided for our basic comforts. You saw we even have board games."

"We didn't play board games in our family."

"That's a shame. We played all the time. Me and Lindsay, Aaron and Elizabeth."

The names sent a chill through Jazz now, like the ghosts in her dreams were clamoring to say their piece about it. So she spoke for them. "Why did you play?"

Stoker fixed his gaze solidly on her. "To connect. To share our lives. To get to know each other better."

"I'm not someone anyone wants to know."

"I want to know."

She met his gaze then and held it. And she found herself wondering for the first time whether maybe she was meant to end up with this man after all. He was old enough to be her father, but he had fed her, bathed her, looked after her. Yes, his son had been a controlling, sadistic asshole, but Stoker himself had never once struck her or threatened to. Except...even though he'd been telling the truth about the bomb, he'd still kept her tied down and played mind games with her far past the point any decent human would have if they'd just been motivated by safety issues.

"I can't," she said at last. "I feel like I'm dead inside. If you opened me up, you'd just see blank pages."

"It's been a shock. Give it time."

"Yeah. I think I'll lie down now." No means *no*, asshole.

"It's early."

"Like I give a fuck."

She pushed away her empty bowl and stumbled to her cot. Just before she lay down, she noted the baseball bat she'd put under her cot was gone. Looking around, she finally saw it lying on the shelf immediately above the board games. Jazz hadn't noticed that during the tour, though it was in clear view. Almost like Stoker was taunting her with it.

She lay down on the cot and closed her eyes.

"Are you going to zip-tie me down?" she called to Stoker.

"Only if you want me to."

Barely audible, she said, "Is that what I tell myself? Fuck."

Then time started to slip for her as she willed herself out of wakefulness. But as she faded in and out, she heard Stoker crank up the radio again and turn the knob through the usual stream of static. Then...were those words through the static? More static. He scribbled in his black book.

Later, a thumping sound from somewhere made Jazz open her eyes enough to see Stoker rise and climb the stairs. He came back down a few beats later.

Later still, she felt the heat of him sitting on the edge of her cot, and his fingers smoothing the hair back from her face.

Which turned into him sitting in the chair halfway between her cot and his with his face in his hands, sobbing.

It woke her up enough to actually open her eyes a slit and watch him walk past her to the where he'd stowed the gun lockbox earlier. He lifted it down and set it on the table near his cot. He dialed it open and took out the Glock.

He aimed it up the stairs.

Then at Jazz.

Then he opened his mouth and stuck the muzzle of the gun into it and closed his eyes.

Jazz closed her own eyes and waited. And waited. And spun into her dreams...

JAZZ SAT UP, wide awake. Panting.

Blackness.

No. Aaron was there, walking down the stairs from the door in his usual dream light.

Which meant she wasn't really awake. Hadn't just awoken. Wasn't panting. This was lucid dreaming. Though the only lucidity involved was her vague knowing it was a dream because she certainly had no control over this SOB walking down the stairs now.

"That was a bit of a kick in the head, hunh?" The SOB, Aaron. "He was telling the truth. At least part of it."

"What?" said Jazz. Said Dream Jazz? Said Jazz talking to herself? "What else is there?"

"The thumping on the door, babe. The voice on the radio. What do you think those are?"

"Other survivors."

Aaron had reached her cot now and climbed over the foot of it. He pushed her back down on the cot so he was lying on top of her, her legs spread so wide under him that the bottom of her dress was up around her waist and Aaron's own crotch pressed into hers.

"And he's not letting the other survivors in, is he?" said Aaron, grinding his crotch against her until she felt her panties getting wet. "Or telling you about them. Why do you think that is?"

"I don't...uh...um...I..."

"You're a pig, Aaron," said Elizabeth. Jazz looked and saw her sitting in her own dream light on the edge of Stoker's cot. "Dad just wants to survive. And keep Jasmine alive. There are limited supplies. And anyone who's out there now is probably burned and dying from radiation anyway."

"And the voice on the radio?" Aaron challenged.

"Someone somewhere. But there's no way to tell from where. It doesn't change the plan. Doesn't change the—"

"Moves!" Aaron crowed, driving his crotch against Jazz's panties again. "They're chess moves. When you both wake up, babe, ask him what his favorite game is. And just remember what one of the main objectives always is."

"Of chess?" Jazz said. "You...uh..."

Lindsay suddenly appeared in her own dream light, shrieking and rampaging across the basement to throw Elizabeth away from her father and grab the hunting knife out of Stoker's sheath and stabbed it into Stoker's back over and over, crying with each thrust. "You capture! The! Queen!"

Then the three ghosts vanished but the dream light lingered on both Jazz and Stoker. His bloody body rolled over and he looked at her, holding out a shaking hand.

Jazz sucked in a cry and the dream light snapped off, leaving her only with blackness and the sound of her own breath, hitching into sobs.

CHAPTER 23

By LATE-AFTERNOON, as identified by Stoker's watch and reinforced by the lantern's steady hiss of light, the night sobs and terrors were forgotten.

More than forgotten. Jazz had actually felt the resurgence of something resembling hope inside her. Enough hope that she'd decided she needed to rebuild the strength she'd lost from her days unconscious, and those spent conscious but tied to her cot.

So she stood by the end of her cot, doing squats with the bottom of her dress torn to allow the movement, touching her cot for balance where needed. She could feel the burn in her quads and the almost giddy rush of dizziness as her body tried to adjust to demanding movement again. The animal inside her roared.

And she didn't even care that Stoker was watching her with more interest than he should.

"I found a box I forgot I had," he said.

"Thirteen...fourteen...fifteen...What's in it?"

Jazz switched to stretching, feeling the sweat trickling

down her face, her back, her armpits. If she still had the ability to smell herself in all this heat and confinement, she suspected she'd gag.

"I found clothes," Stoker said. "Jeans. Tee-shirts. They may be oversized for you, but...."

Jazz stopped her stretching and looked down at the wrinkled, sweaty, dirty disaster she wore that was once her best party dress. That she'd worn to make Aaron happy and maybe, subconsciously, to attract Stoker's eye enough that he'd actually help her get free of Aaron. Well, it had kind of worked exactly like that, hadn't it? And now she couldn't be more ready to change into something else. Anything else.

"Oh my god, yes," she said. "Please."

"Not that you don't look fetching in your ripped party dress and all..."

"Please! I said please."

Stoker walked over behind his cot and returned with a plastic storage box that looked large enough for a couple of kids to hide in. He set it down, took off the lid, and pulled out a pair of jeans and a pastel blue tee-shirt with some kind of design on it. He tossed them to Jazz, who caught them and looked them over.

They were a little big, but if she rolled up the bottom of the jeans, they could work.

"Lindsay's early years," Stoker said.

"Turn your back."

"Really? It's not like I haven't..."

She snapped him a look. "What? You haven't what?"

Stoker shrugged and turned his back.

In the moment of privacy, Jazz whipped off her dress then stood, hesitating, agonizing over whether to keep or throw out her sweat-soaked bra and panties. A look at Stoker's back convinced her to keep them and she quickly tugged on the jeans and tee-shirt, glad of her decision. Because the jeans were a little big and a little rough on the inside. She appreciated the panty buffer. While the tee-shirt was almost tight, the material none too thick. The bra kept down her nipple bumps and gave her an extra layer of protection.

"Okay," she said.

Stoker turned and appraised her carefully, his gaze lingering on her body. "From sexual tramp to survivalist badass," he said. "Almost as good as a bath."

"Ha." She hated that she actually liked his approval.

"Boots here, too, and a backpack. For hiking out. We'll do a dry-run prep in a day or two."

"Be prepared."

"That's right."

And out of nowhere her dream came back to her. "What's your favorite board game?"

But Stoker had switched focus ahead of her. "Before that, I want to talk about something else. Something important."

"What?"

"Blast zone survivors."

"Like us." Jazz laughed uncomfortably. This had also been in the dream. Like Stoker had shared it or read her mind.

"If the survivors out there were like us, they'd be holed up in whatever basement or concrete edifice protected them from the nuclear fire and most of the radiation. No. These are the ones who survived but only barely. They'll probably have third degree burns from the heat blast, maybe infections arising from those, plus radioactive burns and poisoning."

"You think there are survivors like that out there? Near us?"

"You've heard the banging on the door, haven't you? People trying to get in. I lied about things falling against the door. The security bar is to keep any survivors in the area out."

"To die."

And even though she knew it and could see that he knew she knew it, he said, "They're already dead, Jasmine. The only question is whether we let them kill us too."

It made her stomach churn. The banging she'd heard, not once or twice, but every time, it seemed, she'd been about to fall asleep. That was real people, desperate people, who were just trying to survive. Who probably loved and clung to life more than Jazz ever had.

"We could have shared our water with them."

"Our water. Our food. Our minimally-radiated space. Yes, we could have. It probably would have killed us and not helped them beyond an extra week or two of life. But we could have."

"And you called me reptilian."

He walked up to her and feigned a poke at her chest. She jerked backwards to avoid it and he laughed. "We're all reptiles," he said. "The reptile brain knows hunger and fear. It's what keeps us alive. Both of us."

"So what do you want? My blessing?"

He shook his head. "I want you to admit your culpability."

"My what? As in guilt?"

He smiled. "You know the word. Good. Because when we finally walk out of here together, when we reach the people who weren't in the blast zone, when we reach those people, they will ask what every person outside a tragedy asks of those who were inside one—how much did you try to help others?"

"I didn't even—"

"And if you tell them we locked them out, they're going to say we killed them. They'll say that we abandoned them, and when we did that, we abandoned our humanity. So why shouldn't humanity now abandon us?"

"Wait! *I* didn't lock them out!"

He walked past her to look up the stairs. "No. You did nothing. Left alone, you would have simply walked out of here and died of heat and radiation. Or you would have let the walking dead inside and been raped and murdered for the supplies we have here." He whirled on her. "Are you going to tell them that?"

He was right. Oh god. "I... No. I..."

"Jasmine, I don't mean to confuse you. It's very simple. When we walk out of here, out of the blast zone, and reach safety, we simply tell people that we saw no one else. That for all we knew, everyone around us died in the blast."

"But if they ask if I ever heard...

He'd somehow come close to her and now placed his hands on both her arms in reassurance. Or was it control? "You pass the question to me," he said. "We're together now, you and I. We have both lost everyone else and are bound by our survival together. I will never leave you. And you will never leave me. Not to be indelicate, but if you want to ever get out of this alive, those are the terms."

She tried to laugh it off. "What's that, like, a marriage proposal?"

He still held her arms. "Call it what you want. It's survival. It's a non-negotiable term of our little adventure together."

"Holy shit."

"And my favorite board game? Chess. Forgive the obvious, but it always ends in 'mate.'"

She tried to pull away and he tightened his grip on her. It was happening. Now. Despite all his protestations, despite the fact he'd been telling the truth about the nuclear blast, it still came down to this, to him forcing himself on her. Her vision swam for a moment and a little pool of bile shot up the back of her throat.

"What about the radio?" she said now since she had nothing to lose. "I heard a voice on the radio. And you said the fires were dying down. So we can go earlier, right?"

He started running his hands up and down her arms. "Soon, maybe. But I still say when and how we go. Do you understand that, Jasmine? Or do I have to zip tie you to your cot again?"

"No. No, you don't."

One hand had left her arms and run up the side of her neck. Its fingers traced her jaw line to her chin. He touched her lips. "And your agreement to my terms?"

Inside, every internal alarm had started to clang and ring. Her inside animal roared and leapt about in wild frustration. Blood rushed to her face, turning it even hotter than she remembered the air outside being.

And *just as fast*, her self-preserving brain kicked in to analyze all her options, work out a strategy, a plan. She was *not* giving up this time the way she did with Aaron.

"Give me some time to think," she said softly. "Okay?" That endearing female uptick. That question versus statement. "I was just getting used to the idea I could be with someone who wasn't trying to own me. Now, I guess...readjustment."

Which was as close as she could get to a slap in his face and a kick in his balls. Telling him he had almost had her *voluntarily.* (A lie. It had to be.) Now he was just like his asshole son all over again.

But she wasn't even sure Stoker got it as he shrugged, turned, and went over to put the top back on the clothing box.

NIGHT IN THE BASEMENT. No light. Jazz heard only herself breathing, like she was the last soul in the universe. And soon she, too, would be stilled and there would be only a great nothing.

But then she stood. At least she thought she was standing. It felt like a floor under her feet. And when she took a step, it appeared again, that feeling of floor.

She stepped and stepped and reached and found...the bat. It felt like the bat. It jumped into her hands like the bat should, round and wood-grainy, with a knob on the end.

She turned and, not having any idea really which way she was walking, she stepped and stepped, turned, and sat.

On her cot.

As a dream light barely illuminated Elizabeth's torso and face sitting at the foot of Jazz's cot. It also illuminated the baseball bat in Jazz's hands. Was it the same one which Stoker had followed her down with? Which she had swung back and forth and playfully/seriously hinted at swinging against Stoker's head? She couldn't be sure. Nothing in her dream seemed sure this time.

"Well?" she asked Elizabeth.

Knowing that Elizabeth would know exactly what she was asking. Defend your father *now*. Tell me what he's doing *now* if he's so wonderful. Or tell me how to defeat him.

"Okay," Elizabeth said quietly. "But you can't just attack him. Or sneak up on him. He's too smart for that. The only way past his defenses is to let down all of yours. Show him all your secrets. Everything you are."

Jazz felt a rush of panic. "But there's nothing there. Blank pages. I told him."

"Maybe he doesn't believe that. Men rarely do."

Santino suddenly appeared in a dream light behind Elizabeth and cupped her breast with his hands, nuzzling her neck.

"And watch my dad's fingers," Elizabeth said even as she leaned into Santino's nuzzling. "He taps them when he's lying. Did you notice that?"

The dream lights winked out on them but one lingered on Jazz as she lay down on her bed and rolled away from Stoker's side of the room so she could carefully clank the bat just under the cot.

Then her light too was gone so there was only blackness.

And Jazz breathing.

CHAPTER 25

BREAKFAST.

Jazz sat in the chair behind the radio table, silently eating her bowl of porridge. On the floor nearby, the plastic clothes container was open again. Beside it sat the pair of women's hiking boots and socks that Jazz had tried on first thing after her morning pee. While Stoker had been heating the porridge.

The boots had fit decently. Certainly better than going barefoot through the fires and rubble or picking through them in high heels.

Stoker, meanwhile, wore a flak jacket and sat on the edge of his cot sharpening his hunting knife. He scraped it down over and over on the light blue whetstone that lay on the sheeted mattress of the cot.

On the radio table were food rations and two water bottles. Also a compass and flashlight. A backpack sat on the floor, propped against a table leg.

Jazz finished her breakfast and considered carefully before she spoke.

"So I've been thinking."

Stoker paused his scraping. "Yes?" he said.

"There's an element of fate in all of this."

"How so?"

She gave what she hoped was an accepting smile. "I chose your class. I chose your son. But choosing Aaron really just got me closer to you."

Stoker ran his finger along both flat edges of his hunting knife, as he said, "Arguing from an end condition, everything appears to be fate."

"I may be pregnant with his child."

Stoker stopped dead and looked at her. "With Aaron's child?"

Jazz nodded. "I did a pregnancy test the afternoon before we came to your house. Assuming it's accurate..."

"My god."

She made another stab at a smile. "Despite everything I said to you, that I accused you of, that I'm...afraid of, I want my baby to have a father."

It was almost funny how much the cool aloofness Stoker had worn all morning melted into something like syrup. He sheathed his knife and picked up the whetstone. "Of course. Of course you do."

He put the whetstone near the other survival supplies on the table then came around it, tugged her chair so she faced sideways from the table and knelt beside her. He tentatively held his hand over her stomach.

"May I...?"

Jazz grimaced. "There's nothing there yet. Not even a bump. I just feel fat."

"Can I do it anyway?"

She shrugged and forced herself to smile like it was no big deal. Stoker put his hand on her belly through the tee-shirt, moving it about and rubbing it gently in such an intimate way she half expected him to go for her breasts or crotch.

But just as she was about to say something, she froze. His fingers had started to tap her belly. Like he was trying to test it for hollowness? Trying to wake up the child inside? Or like he was not even aware he was doing it because all his focus was on how deftly he was about to lie.

"You know what I said yesterday about you not making it out alive if you didn't stick with me? That was hyperbole."

Oh shit. Jazz knew he meant it last night. Now she knew he still meant it this morning. He was ready to kill her if it came to that.

But what she said was, "You meant we have to stick together. I got that. Even more than you know." She indicated her belly. "But it works both ways."

"What do you mean?"

"You're asking me to commit to you, with no more games, while you hide things from me."

"Like what?"

And here she was treading on dangerous ground. Her subconscious had told her she had to get inside his defenses, totally expose herself to him and have him trust her completely. That was the only way she'd get the opening she needed to escape him. So she had to go deep, cut for the heart and be ready to bleed out for him in the same way.

"You talked a few days ago," she inched into it, "about how you'd lost so much, even before you met me. That it would explain everything and tell me how this all had to end."

He shook it off and removed his hand from her belly, placing it on her thigh instead. "Hyperbole."

"Was it?"

His fingers were still. Time for truth.

"Okay," he said, "let's say there was a professor..."

"You."

"...and a grad student."

"Name?"

"Irrelevant. Call her Mandy."

"Oh, Mandy."

"And the professor and grad student spent more time together than they should have and it became sexual."

"Romantic as well?" Jazz asked.

Stoker's fingers started tapping again, this time on Jazz's upper thigh. How could he not see that? "Not on my part, but on hers. Which is why, of course, I had to break it off. She couldn't handle it. She began stalking me. Insisting we get back together. She needed me so much."

*Tap. Tap. Tap.*

"And your wife found out," Jazz said.

"I confessed to my wife. I came clean about how this girl had seduced me and that it meant nothing to me. We had to go to court to get a restraining order against her."

He'd tapped irregularly through that. Either he was getting spastic or telling half truths or the tapping was only an approximate guide to when he was speaking the truth. But even as Jazz feigned sympathy with an, "Oh my God," Stoker's fingers went completely still. A clear truth coming up.

"Lindsay, of course, shut me out of our bed. Threatened divorce."

Duh. "That part I believe."

"Pardon me?"

"I spoke with her while we made dessert. She was still angry."

The tapping started up again.

"Which was so sad," Stoker sighed. "It was one time. It had never happened before then."

"And you loved your wife."

The tapping stopped.

"I did. You can't imagine how much."

"As you will love me."

"If you will let me. Over time. Love will grow. I will be a father to your child. I will cherish you and provide for you. We will start a new family."

Jazz looked to his fingers. They were dead still. Which meant a) he'd had affairs with a lot of young women; b) he had dearly loved his wife, and c) he planned to or already did, love Jazz. The sickness of it in light of his tying her up and threatening to kill her, made her stomach turn into one roiling lump and she leaned over her knees, choking.

He drew out his hand from her thigh and rubbed her back. "Jasmine?"

"I'm...I'm maybe even more pregnant than I thought."

Stoker hopped up and retrieved the chair from the other side of the table. He placed it directly beside hers and sat thigh-to-thigh with her, pulling her close to him, stroking her hair. And as much from exhaustion and fear as from calculation, Jazz sank into him. She gave herself over to the fantasy that he really was kind and loving and simply comforting her like a good friend or gentle lover would.

It obviously stirred something in him, too. He leaned his face down into her hair and breathed into it, whispering, "You're still trying to trick me, aren't you."

"No tricks," she murmured back. "Negotiation. I'm negotiating with my heart."

"By telling me you're pregnant? Interesting." But he still held her as he said it. His gentle embrace, his cheek to her hair belied the intellectualism.

"And my dreams," Jazz said into his chest. "Do you know who I talk with each night in my dreams? Your son and daughter. And Santino. Lindsay. Trying to explain you to me. Or explain me to myself. Do you see how sad that is? That even in my dreams I can't call up my dead family, only yours?"

"What did they say?"

"Elizabeth." Jazz sighed. "I think she loved you the most. She told me...to let myself trust you."

"Her ghost told you that? Or your subconscious?"

She pulled back for a moment to look up into his face. "I don't know. I don't know anything anymore. Except that I'm defeated. And scared. And tired of fighting. Being on guard all the time—it's exhausting."

"I know," he said, eyes serious. "I know that. For me too."

"So, if I could just trust you... If you could just trust me..."

"Please. Yes."

She sank back against his chest and then reached her hand up to the opening at the top of his shirt. "So tell me what's on the chain around your neck."

Stoker's hand whipped suddenly from her hair to the hand on his chest. Then he relaxed and pulled her up to a full sitting position beside him.

"A trade then," he said. "I show you what I have on my chain, you give me one kiss."

"I..." She looked in alarm at his eyes but didn't see lust there, only a deep deep need. And Jazz understood all at once that, however morally weak and misguided Stoker clearly was, he was also a hopeless romantic who needed to be needed, needed to love and be loved. And he'd lost all of his family. He had only Jazz. And was giving her now the opportunity to do now exactly what her unconscious in the form of Elizabeth had told her to do—give her whole self to him openly.

She licked her lips nervously. "Okay. Agreed. As long as you go first."

CHAPTER 26

STOKER'S HANDS went to the buttons of his shirt. He normally had the top two unbuttoned. He undid two more, then reached in and pulled out the bottom of the chain Jazz earlier seen glinting there.

A locket.

It was oval, like a smooth gold skipping stone in Stoker's hand.

As Jazz watched, Stoker fumbled it open to reveal a small family photo of Stoker, Lindsay, and a young Aaron and Elizabeth.

"Aaron was five when this was taken," Stoker said. "Elizabeth was eight. We'd just driven back from Disneyland. Long drive. And I remember just before we got home and took this, I looked in the rear view mirror and saw Aaron sniffing his armpits. Like this."

Stoker lifted his left arm and craned his nose down that way to sniff the armpit. Then his right arm.

"And he sighs and says, looking out the window, 'They smell like roses in the summertime.'"

Jazz smiled. "Seriously."

Stoker nodded. "I shit you not. It's one of my favorite memories of him. A sweet, innocent kid with a poetic soul."

It was like Jazz's understanding of the world was melting like the pavement outside had melted and reformed. "I saw...moments of that," she said.

"Sometimes we only get moments."

Did he know? Did he understand what his son had become? Did any of that truly matter now that Aaron was gone? That her entire past life, with all its dreams, hopes, and fears, was gone?

Jazz felt herself tearing up as she said, "But you saved that one moment. Kept it right by your heart."

Stoker nodded, kissed the picture, then closed the locket and slid it back inside the front of his shirt, automatically re-buttoning the two buttons he'd undone to take it out.

"The world order may be harsh, Jasmine," he said. "But there is good in it also. Which why you need to look for it. Find the beauty in others. And if you're fortunate enough to find someone filled with beauty and also a great need you can fill, you overlook the flaws of circumstance, age, background, and embrace the opportunity. As I have with you."

He reached a finger up to stroke Jazz's jaw like he had the night before. But this time it was with tenderness, not possession, and he searched her eyes as he did it, asking her permission. Which Jazz felt her whole being offering to him instinctively. Whether from a recognition of his need and her own need to be needed, or just as payment somehow for the way he had loved his family. Because such a beautiful love should be rewarded.

His hands snuck around the back of her neck, fingers reaching into her hair, before he pulled her lips to his with a gentle but insistent pressure. Jazz, for all her wanting to give in, for all the sense of inevitability of it, resisted for a moment, even as their lips touched.

His were dry, narrow, surrounded by prickly grizzle. He probably tasted bad, but the feeling of scum she'd had in her own mouth for days now made it hard to tell. She could smell his sweat and body odor like she smelled her own, just part of the basement. Part of their world.

Then she gave in to the pressure and their lips joined completely in full feeling. He turned his head and they slid together even more.

He didn't stick his tongue into her. He didn't grind against her. He just moved his lips and jaw to feel her. To *feel*. And she couldn't help but answer. Her heart was thumping hard. Racing. He was kissing her and she, him. *Feeling*, in the midst of all this madness.

He pulled back slightly and she took the cue, separating with a gentle, wet sound.

But only an inch or two. Their lips hovered close to each other.

"I...want...to trust," Jazz whispered.

"Then let go," Stoker said. "I won't let you fall."

Jazz's heart raced, pounding so hard it in her ears it made it hard to think. But she had to think now. She was *in*. This was happening. Their coming together was *on*. Which meant a chance. If she could just think...

She threw herself into another kiss, less gentle this time, her mouth moving and sucking, her tongue seeking his.

It made his hands snake around her, pulling her close to him, even as she wrapped her arms around the back of his neck and plunged her fingers into his hair.

The heat! God, the heat! Of their bodies. Of the room.

The chairs were scraping and moving under them as her dragged her torso against his. As he pulled his lips off her mouth and kissed his way down her neck. His left hand swept from her back and up her front, grabbing her breast through her clothes. His other hands swept down and up under her tee-shirt, feeling her sweaty back, her bare skin, finding her bra.

"Oh....no. My bed," she gasped. "My cot. Not here."

His hands came back to her face and he kissed her again, then stood up. He took her hands to pull her to her feet but, before she could walk with him, leaned and swept her up off her feet. Like a new bride, he carried her across the basement to her cot. There he set her gently down to sit on the edge of it. And before she was even settled, he grabbed the bottom of her tee-shirt, dragging it up and over her head, with Jazz complying as if it was exactly her plan, too.

Stoker took a step back and drank in the sight of her then, smiling like a lustful child. He began stripping off his flak jacket. His shirt. Button. Button. Button...

Jazz lay back sideways over her cot and reached for where her dream self had left the baseball bat.

It wasn't there!

She looked to where it had been on the shelf above the games yesterday. Not there either!

Now Stoker's shirt was off and he was all over her, trying to get her jeans down.

"No!" she blurted and grabbed his hair, making him freeze. "I mean, no. Don't rush it. It should be special. Let me make it special. I've wanted this so badly. Let me do you first."

She rolled her body up as he took a step back. Her fingers went to his belt, pulling out the strap, tugging it out of the metal fastener and free. Then the pants fastener, a hook and bar closure that she fumbled with a little because Aaron had always worn jeans and button fronts.

She needn't have worried as Stoker's fingers shot in to help her and a second later his pants had dropped around his ankles, along with the sheathed hunting knife. He kicked off his shoes furiously, his erection straining and bobbing about under his shorts as he did.

Finally he was done and stood before her, breathing heavily, in just his boxers.

"All right," Jazz breathed. She ran a hand up his bare leg and squeezed his erection through the boxers. "Now lie down, Professor. And close your eyes. Let your prize pupil show you how it's done."

She stood and saw his eyes were almost glassy as he obeyed like a slave. He sat on the cot and turned to lie lengthwise...

...as Jazz furiously used one hand to pull the pile of his pants and belt from beside his shoes. She found the knife sheath and unclipped it. She had to use both hands to draw out the hunting knife and grip its wood-and-metal-butt handle tightly so the knife stuck up at a right angle to her arm.

Stoker, no doubt wondering what was taking her so long, raised up his head and she swung the knife butt at his temple.

CHAPTER 27

THE KNIFE BUTT connected with a thud, snapping Stoker's head to the side. And down. The temple streamed blood. Stoker was out cold.

Dead?

No. Breathing. Better than Jazz was at that moment.

"Okay, move," she ordered herself. "Jazz, move. Knife sheath. Check. Shirt on. Good. Socks. Get the damn socks." She sprinted across the room in her bare feet for the boots and socks she'd tried on earlier. Tugged on the socks in a panic. "Good. Now boots. Okay. Tie fast, tighten later. Where's the backpack?"

It was on the floor near Stoker's cot. She scooped it up and took it to the table where she started throwing in everything she saw there—the sharpening stone, a compass, a map, empty water bottles. Then she was back to the food shelves where she started throwing rations into her pack— peanut butter, nuts, dried fruit, cereal bars, anything that was light and ready to eat. And then to a water barrel, turning the spigot, filling her three water bottles. Everything into her backpack.

"Water. Food. Knife. He's still out. Go, go, go!"

She was still slinging the backpack on her back as she ran for the stairs and up. At the top, she crouched down to bang up and push at the upper 2x4 safety bar until it came free. She used her boots to kick up the bottom one, then grabbed it and yanked it upwards. She tossed both of them down the stairs behind her.

Then she pulled out the hunting knife and repeated the procedure she'd watched Stoker go through. Saw open the duct tape along the bottom. A full three feet this time so she could be sure of squeezing out the door. Then she sawed down vertically.

She missed the line Stoker had cut before and so had to saw a double or triple layer of duct tape. It got messy. Her hammering heart made her want to just grab the covering and rip and tear it off, but a lingering sound of her father talking about the dangers of fiberglass, how it got in your fingers as well as you nose and lungs. She should have found some gloves, damn it!

But she was on the top line across, sawing as the thick cover of fiberglass popped away from the tape with each cut. One more long cut and...

Argh. Her shoe lace.

She hadn't tied it properly or stepped on it in her haste. She ducked down to give it quick re-tie and one of the 2x4s she'd tossed down the stairs moments banged into the door over her head and fell down onto her back.

Stoker!

Jazz threw off the board and whirled around with her knife out, but Stoker, still in just his boxers, his left temple running with blood, was already up the stairs and grabbed her wrist. He twisted it so hard and fast she cried out in pain and dropped the knife. He scooped it up and dragged her down the stairs as she kicked and beat at him. But even over her snarls and screams, his damn voice cut through like the practiced presenter he was.

"This is a student who showed such promise, but is obviously in need of some remedial attention."

They reached the bottom of the stairs and he spun her around, ripped off her backpack, and held her from behind, both of her arms trapped, the hunting knife in his hand pressed up against her face. Her panic spiked. Her vision went red.

"Should it be corporal punishment?" Stoker went on to his imaginary classroom. "Certainly not. Though I suspect paddling her bottom might be highly enjoyable. No, I believe only a face-to-face confrontation with total honestly will do."

He half-carried, half-dragged her backwards to her cot, then spun her to face him again and slapped her hard across her face.

It shocked her into stillness for a second, but as Stoker reached out his hands to grab and cut off her shirt, Jazz punched him with all her might across the side of his face.

He staggered back, tripped on Jazz's cot, and landed on his ass. He hadn't lost the knife, though.

"Stupid bitch," he spat, glaring at her.

But Jazz wasn't looking at him. She was seeing how his tumbling fall had shoved over her cot and revealed that she actually had hidden the baseball bat under it after all. It had just rolled far enough under that she hadn't been able to reach it earlier.

Now, as Stoker shook off his second blow to the head and started to rise, Jazz ran and dived at the bat. She scooped it up, then jumped up and danced around Stoker, backing her way along the shelves in the direction of his cot, looking for a place to make her stand.

Stoker sneered and stalked after her with his knife in front of him, ready to slice or stab.

Jazz raised her bat and dug it into the supply shelves, sweeping their contents out onto the floor between her and Stoker. Books, dishes and pots, cutlery clattered. Bags and boxes of rice and beans, pudding cups, shredded and sprayed everywhere. Jazz leapt back towards Stoker just enough to swing hard at the water spigots of his two plastic canisters, knocking them off so that water streamed out into the entire mess.

"You cunt!" Stoker screamed as he slipped and hopped in his bare feet through it all.

Then he was close enough and lunged directly for her with the knife.

Jazz cracked the bat down across his forearm so hard that he spun around and went down, losing the knife. Jazz lunged for it and scooped it up in her free hand but Stoker had scrambled up right behind her and grabbed her around the waist.

She swung the knife down. Nicked his thigh, drawing blood.

Then he had her knife arm, twisting it up painfully behind her.

"Drop it!" he said. "Now!"

With a cry of pain, she let it fall.

"And the bat!"

With a last wild attempt, she spun half out of Stoker's grasp and swung the bat for his head. But he ducked and it swished over him in a wide circle that pulled her off balance. Stoker rose up and punched her jaw.

Jazz's head spun and she crumpled, vision blurry. She ordered her body to roll up but it ignored her.

"As I was saying," Stoker wheezed, "it's finally time for a face-to-face confrontation with total honesty. Ready or not."

Stoker half knelt and scooped Jazz up. He staggered back to her cot with her and dropped her there. With awful focus, he stripped off her boots and socks, shirt and jeans, then sliced off her bra and panties so she lay groggy and naked.

He removed his own boxers and climbed on top of her.

THE YOUNG WOMAN interviewing Stoker was beginning to understand how Stoker's face had become so incredibly ravaged—covered with burns, cuts, scrapes, and bruises. But she also saw his eyes were as sharp as when he'd begun his story, eagerly sizing up how she was handling it.

"You remember my question?" he said. "A female rat was in a maze with no exit. Male rat was put in with her. What do you think happened? Now you know. They fucked each others' brains out."

The young woman shifted in her seat, sweating in the confines of this secure room mere feet from this monster. She ground her pen hard onto her clipboard to help her keep her professional remove, but couldn't help saying, "It doesn't sound like they...fucked each other," she said. "More like it was one way."

Stoker gave her a twisted smile. "Oh, it was both ways, believe me. Both rats got fucked. Just not at the same time."

CHAPTER 29

THE RAPE WAS horrible and surreal for Jazz.

She had so long dreaded it, imagined it, fought to elude it, that it was like a living thing inside her before it happened. And she expected to dissociate, go somewhere else in her mind when it happened, as she'd heard many rape victims did. As she'd done herself when sex with Aaron had turned mean and violent.

She was wrong.

She was fully present as Stoker entered her. As his hands pawed and slapped and choked her. As he tossed her around and flipped her over and back like she was a piece of meat. She saw flashes of his face, a mask of rage, blood oozing from his temple. Then the lumpy pillow of her cot, the shelves, jerking and thumping about in her vision. She felt his hands, his ragged fingernails, his dick. Tasted bile and dust, sweat, tears, blood. There was no love here. No romantic need. No *person* at all. Just a beast.

When it was over, though, a small, bitter nub inside her thanked God that at least Stoker had enough social chains that even when driven to this savagery, he had not used his knife or brutalized her with anything but himself.

He slid his sweaty, bloody body off hers and staggered to his feet. He splatted onto the receding wide puddle that had splashed out of the water canisters faster than it could drain through the basement's drain and was only now down to a final *drip, drip, drip.* He found his wet clothes and knife. Swore and carried them, bare feet splashing, to his own cot. Dumped his package there.

"Nothing sexist in this, Jasmine," he croaked as he gingerly examined his temple. "Just an atavistic urge to fuck. For tomorrow we many die. When we go forth. Since we *have* to go forth now that you've ruined most of our supplies."

He managed to pull on his underwear before his weakness overcame him and he fell onto his cot, moaning.

Jazz, her head turned to the side, watched all of this, then took a ragged breath. She lay on her back, limbs splayed out, too shaken to even curl into the fetal position she so wanted to hide in. Or maybe it was that a part of her knew if she did curl up like that, it was game over.

She had been defeated, brutalized, beaten down into nothing. And yet...

She twitched her toes, her fingers, her limbs, her hips. It hurt to breathe and she knew it would hurt more to move, but she knew she *could* move. And her survival mind, because she had not dissociated herself from the deed, was still fully alive in her.

Stoker's eyes closed.

Fighting the urge to cry out or run, Jazz carefully studied the rest of the space between her and Stoker. The pots and pans and boxes and cans on the floor. The soggy mess of rice and flour and water.

And the little league baseball bat.

It lay where Stoker had made her drop it over by the food shelves.

Jazz quieted her breathing and carefully, clenching her teeth against the pain, rolled off the cot onto her hands and knees onto the slowly draining and evaporating sheen of water. She pulled on her wet jeans and shirt. Then she stood and walked as quietly as she could to the baseball bat, watching Stoker as she did.

He didn't register her approach until she actually picked up the bat in both hands, then the small scratch of it or a sixth sense made him open his eyes and groan his way up to sitting. His hand fumbled for his knife, but he wasn't wearing his pants. He found the pile of wet things he'd dumped on his cot a few minutes earlier. Pulled out the knife and...

*CRACK!*

Jazz's bat, swung with all the strength she had left, caught him across the side of the head again and he went down onto the cot almost where he'd been before. Lay still.

Jazz stood watching him carefully for what seemed like a two full minutes, her bat cocked to swing again. When he didn't move, she stepped in close and checked his pulse and breathing.

Alive.

She shook her head in disbelief. "You are one tough sonofabitch, Professor."

She positioned the baseball bat up over his head and raised it high. Paused. Breathed hard in and out.

Lowered it again.

"Atavistic, reptilian bullshit." She spat at him. "I don't fear you anymore. But I don't trust you either, you...you raping father of Aaron. Even when you're bleeding and half dead."

She stepped carefully back to the shelves and found the zip ties he'd been using on her during their first days down here. She went back to Stoker, lifted his legs up onto his cot, spread the ankles, and zip tied them tightly onto the bottom side and end rails. Then his wrists, above his head, tied to the cot corners.

When he was fully secured, she tracked down the hiking boots and socks she'd tried on before breakfast. The boots had been upright and the socks stuffed inside them so they were amazingly dry. She brought them back to her cot, dried her feet on the mattress sheet, and put on the boots. Standing up in them gave her an immediate shot of energy.

She saw the backpack on the ground at the bottom of the stair. Dry, also. She could just grab that and leave now.

"No, Jazz," she whispered. "Come on. No immediate threat. Think it through."

Nodding to herself, she went back to Stoker and calmly retrieved his knife and its sheath. She clipped the sheath to her waistband and slid the knife into it.

She took Stoker's watch and stuffed it into her jeans pocket.

Retrieved the baseball bat as well.

She did a more careful hunt around the radio where she'd taken the compass and flashlight from earlier. This time she stopped at his little black book, where he'd presumably stored information about things he'd heard on the shortwave radio. She grabbed it, along with the pen and was about to just stuff it into her back when she decided to open it at random. Just to see the sort of things he'd recorded.

She read and her face drained of blood.

She put down her bat, sat at the table, and opened the book to the first page. She began to read.

CHAPTER 30

JAZZ WAS HALFWAY through the book when she heard a groan from behind her. Then Stoker's voice.

"You haven't left yet. Good. Smart girl."

She looked at him with disgust. "You kept a diary? Here I thought you were tracking sounds on the radio, keeping track of our supplies, plotting a route out of here. Mr. Survival. But no. You were engaged in mental masturbation the whole time."

"That's a little harsh." He tugged at his bonds as he said it, confirming he was trapped.

"Is it?" Jazz said. She read: "'J continues to deny the inevitability of our union. But the fact I didn't take advantage of her when she was unconscious has her questioning her resistance. Her lips when she looks at me in question... God, her lips!'"

"They're pretty lips," Stoker said. "Keep talking. Good things happen when you talk."

His face looked feverish and the blood streaked down and crusted from his head wound make him look like some kind of battle-mad ghoul. Or a zombie. Or someone turning into a zombie. Sure. It was that kind of end-of-the-world scenario, wasn't it?

It was also just the scenario of an older guy who'd been perving on her close up for over a week now.

"How would you have described the rest of me after today?" Jazz said. "Or is the excitement all gone now that you got what you wanted?"

Stoker looked suddenly so sad he might cry. "I didn't get what I wanted, though, did I? Love's hardly as sweet when it's taken by force."

Jazz laughed. "Love?"

"Yes, Jasmine. However badly, I—"

"You've done that before, haven't you?"

"I haven't." He shook his head so hard that she had to check his fingers. No tapping. Telling the truth. "That's the odd thing. Every other student, and Lindsay, they all loved me desperately for a time. They gave themselves willingly. And I didn't love them half as intensely as I love you."

"You're a psychopath," Jazz said. "You're worse than Aaron was."

He shook his head. "Sociopath, if anything, Jasmine. Be precise. Psychopaths don't form close attachments. And my life is all about close attachments."

"You're going to have a close attachment to your cot for the rest of it."

She stood and shoved the black book and pen into her backpack. Put it on. She picked up the baseball bat and turned to leave.

Stoker called out quickly, "I hope you read my speculations about the other survivors out there? I mean, if you are going."

Jazz looked back. "You told me. Other people. Horribly burned, dying, whatever."

"Who aren't trying to reach help outside the blast zone? Why not?"

She shrugged. "Too injured to walk?"

"Yet they keep coming back to our door and pounding on it. At night mostly. You know what that tells me? What I think happened? I think the healthiest blast survivors holed up like us or already tried to escape the blast zone. Others just went crazy and reverted to their basest natures. They skulk and hide during the day. They forage for fresh water and food at night. Probably kill others for territory. Maybe eat them."

Jazz laughed at him. "You've watched too many movies."

Stoker shook his head, his face serious as if he was teaching her in class again and he was disappointed by her lack of comprehension. "I'm merely taking the facts we know. There are people out there who want what we have. And who know we've denied them. I lied when I said you couldn't hear anything through the door. I've heard them screaming at me to let them in. And cursing me. That's what you're going to face when you leave this place. By yourself. Armed with a baseball bat and a knife."

"I wasn't even—"

"Even if they don't figure you were in here with me, just remember that women in a war zone are usually seen as spoils. Property."

Jazz felt herself frowning, thinking through what he'd said and finding no fundamental flaws in the reasoning. Then her mind clicked through their time together. Other supplies. Her eyes shot to the lockbox on the top survival shelf.

"The gun..." she said.

He nodded. "Smart girl. Release me and I'll get it. I'll get dressed and we'll head out of here together."

Jazz glared at him, then walked over and put the edge of the hunting knife to his throat. "Just tell me the combination on the lockbox."

He didn't even blink. "If you were going to kill me, you would have done it already. And torture? You don't have it in you, Jasmine. You're going to be a mother. You're meant to nurture. I'm meant to protect you."

She pressed down on the knife until the blood started, until Stoker's breath hitched, then she drew back, shrugged, sheathed the knife, and walked over to retrieve the lockbox. She brought it back to a patch of floor near the bottom of the stairs that was still dry and set it down. Then lined up the baseball bat over it. Raised the bat...

"You know anything about guns, Jasmine?" Stoker called out. "Like how if you bend the firing pin, they can explode in your face when you fire them?"

Jazz lowered the bat, turned and looked at him. With one booted foot, she kicked the lockbox away from her. "Whoever's out there? They don't want me. They want you and your supplies. They can have them."

So saying, she stepped to the stairs and climbed them. At the top, she took out the knife again and finished cutting through the top of the door covering. She re-sheathed the knife.

Down in the basement, Stoker yell up at her, "Don't be stupid, Jasmine! Ms. Kazmi! Whoever's out there will take your pack, your weapons, then... Take me with you! YOU CANNOT DO THIS ALONE!"

Using the baseball bat to push back the fiberglass from the door handle, set down the bat, grabbed the knob, turned it, then lifted a foot up to brace one the doorframe and pulled with all her might. The door scraped a couple inches and jerked to a stop. Jazz almost lost her grip and her adrenaline spiked in fear as she imagined herself tumbling down the stairs. She reset, tugged, strained, grunted, and it scraped inwards some more.

Then it seemed to give way all at once, swinging wide so she had to step back and down a stair.

Jazz stepped back to the top landing, picked up the baseball bat, and adjusted her backpack.

She stepped outside.

CHAPTER 31

THE LANDSCAPE she'd glimpsed five days earlier lay before her in smoking ruins.

Whereas before it had been fire and heat, all feverish destruction and wind, now it was mostly charcoal and ash. Warm, not hot. And the sky was smoky, but the wind had settled into an uneasy shifting in the air so that the layers of ash on the ground moved and settled, moved and settled, like an unhappy race of sea creatures.

Jazz could still hear fires and see them in every direction, but they were sporadic. It was as if a mad arsonist had burned the place down, then come through a second time trying to light whatever was left, but hampered by the sea creatures lapping at his feet.

She stepped through the ash and rubble until she was clear of the mass near the basement door. Then she turned and saw the remains of the Stoker house, such as they were. That the door structure remained was pretty much a miracle as the house around it had been half blown down, then burned into a mass of charred-black beams and masses.

The twisted pipes wrapped around the basement door might have helped. Jazz didn't know.

For a moment she considered walking back into the remains of the house to look for skeletons, but couldn't find it in her heart to do so. The only remains she might have said goodbye to were Elizabeth's. The rest were better left far behind her.

So she turned, took off her backpack, and pulled out her compass. She opened it and moved it around, but it just swung erratically like it was ruined or something in the blast had set up some competing sources of magnetism. Useless.

She chucked it back into her pack anyway, re-donned the pack, and looked around. She thought she almost had her bearings when she picked out what looked like a crest of mountains through the smoke.

Okay, then. That way.

She began to walk.

"How did you get out, then?" asked the young woman interviewing Stoker. Then cursed herself as she heard her Irish accent surfacing. Stress. From current events. From the way Stoker manipulated her emotions. The way he'd manipulated Jasmine.

"You want to know about me?" he said, lifting a charred eyebrow with a smile. "It's not my story."

"But you're here. Of course it's your story also. How did you get out?"

Stoker sighed. "All right. We'll break the point of view convention this one time, or two or three, perhaps, to round things out. Will that satisfy you?"

"How did you get out?"

CHAPTER 33

STOKER LAY TIED HIS COT, staring at the ceiling, enraged.

"You really have to wonder about students these days," he said.

With a mighty upwards pop of his body, he made the cot hop towards the mess of items Jazz had spilled onto the floor earlier.

He made it hop again.

And again.

Then, as one cot leg seemed to catch on a crack in the concrete floor, he wrenched the cot sideways with all his might and made the cot tip over onto its side with a creaking crash.

"Goddamn it!" His right hand. It was now on the floor. It felt like it had almost been sliced off when he toppled the bed over that way.

But he'd landed close enough to where he needed to be. With a few more body pops and wriggling, he managed to close his right hand around a paring knife, one of the many utensils Jasmine had so conveniently knocked to the floor and left for him to retrieve now.

After five minutes of fumbling and cutting himself along with the plastic zip tie, Stoker had his right hand free. It was only a matter of time and grunting pain before he worked his way through the other bonds and fell in a mostly-naked mash onto the soggy basement floor.

"I almost don't want to get dressed now," he muttered to the wet concrete his face pressed into. "So much work."

But there were post-apocalyptic cannibals to avoid and a recalcitrant lover to catch, so it was up and at 'em.

Stoker picked himself up with a determined groan and went looking for some dry clothes.

CHAPTER 34

ON A BURNED-OUT street with no name, Jazz moved carefully from building to building, deeply shadowed husk to husk. It felt like a main street edging the suburb. Commercial buildings. More concrete construction, so more walls still standing. Some were almost complete structures, however hollowed out and blackened by fire.

She thought she kept seeing shapes between piles of rubble and peeking out of twisted metal cars. Elizabeth? Aaron?

Of course that made no sense because she was fully awake and there was still another hour or two of daylight. Maybe. The smoke made everything closer to the darkening gloom of a Seattle drizzle. Which made her realize she dreaded the rain now. Because wouldn't it bring down any of the floating, irradiated particles? Or were they already down? Or was she already breathing them in and being radiated to death herself?

Stoker had seemed to think the radiation wouldn't kill them this long after the blast if the wind was pushing stuff south and she headed east to the mountains. But could she trust his knowledge of radiation any more than his ethical stance on raping his students?

As another face seemed to appear and disappear into the shadows of a building across the street, Jazz decided either she was being followed or she was going crazy. Neither was good.

She pulled Stoker's watch out of her pocket, squinted at it, and realized it was almost eight p.m. She needed to look for a place to camp for the evening. Someplace safe, if there was such a thing.

CHAPTER 35

STOKER, dressed now in combat fatigues, his flak jacket, and hiking boots, dropped in through the window of a burned out building and paused. Listening.

Someone was following him, he was sure. He'd seen faces duck out of shadows, draw back in behind piles of rubble. But he doubted they had weapons or organization. They were probably underfed and barely alive. So as long as he kept moving, he'd stay ahead of them.

Unlike, say, Jasmine chances of staying ahead of him.

Stoker knew how she thought, so he knew which way she'd go. And he'd seen her boot prints. He couldn't be that far behind her. When she settled down for the evening in some place she considered safe, he'd find her.

A sound behind him.

Stoker spun around, pulling and aiming the Glock .45 he'd taken from the lockbox. No safety but the requirement you pull the trigger all the way. Commit to the kill. Stoker had no trouble with that.

But there was nothing there. Just shifting rubble. Or even a crackle from one of the many fires still burning in pockets of this destroyed suburb. And fire was only a threat now to the stupid.

He stuck the pistol back into the pocket of his flak jacket and loped out through the door opposite his entry window.

He had a runaway to catch.

CHAPTER 36

THE BUILDING JAZZ chose to settle down in for the night wasn't the smallest of spaces, but that was for good reason. This burned-out space might have been a good twenty by fifty feet. A store of some kind, she figured, with all the interior walls gone. But it didn't look like it could burn any further because the walls and floor were concrete and it still had much of its roof.

The other selling point was it had only one door but lots of windows. If someone came after her here, she could escape that way, that way, that way...

So Jazz settled down in a darkly-shadowed corner where she figured she'd be all but invisible, just her and her backpack. And baseball bat. And knife.

She listened to the creak of the burned interior timbers up on what had once been the second floor. And the sound of the wind that was picking up. The louder crackling and occasional pop of a persistent fire the next building over. There must have been a stockpile of tires, logs, or something, that was just determined not to go out.

A movement in the far corner across from her!

Jazz stiffened, then quietly drew the flashlight out of her backpack. She clicked it on, moved it around, and saw a black cat ambling towards her.

Then the young daughter of Stoker's neighbors. What was her name? Annie. Around four years old. But what—?

"That's my cat," Annie said.

"Is it?"

The cat had reached Jazz and now rubbed against her leg. Annie walked up right behind it so she stood right in front of Jazz, looking up at her. The girl had tangled hair, a dirty face and arms and hands and clothes, but innocent eyes. Remarkably healthy looking.

"I'm Annie," she said. "What are you doing?"

"Just settling down for the night, Annie. Where are you parents?"

"Right here," said a male voice behind Jazz. Strong hands grabbed her. A hood plunged down over her head and drew tight. She couldn't breathe. No air. Vision going grey.

"We're so sorry," said a woman's voice.

And Jazz lost consciousness.

CHAPTER 37

JAZZ WOKE up hogtied and gagged on the floor in what looked like the same room that she'd been in before. But now it was some kind of camp.

A collection of small fires in a ten-by-ten foot ring around Jazz lit her and the immediate space. Beyond the fires were dark piles of junk—steel barrels, shopping carts, metal shelves—that looked arranged as shooting blinds or hiding places. And walking among them were dark figures Jazz could barely make out. Though, of course, they could all see her.

Her backpack and bat were gone. So were her knife and knife sheath. And freedom. Again.

Where was the little girl?

At that thought, a horribly scarred male stepped into the circle and squatted almost directly before her face. For all his facial distortions, he looked familiar.

"Hello, Jasmine," he said. "I'm assuming you're Jasmine. We read the black book you carried in your pack, my wife and me. It's pretty hard to mistake the stuffed-up, egocentric tone of our favorite neighbor. What an asshole. But he sure liked you."

A woman stepped into view immediately behind him. She had horrible burns on her face and arms, but was clearly the woman Jazz remembered holding her young daughter, Annie, that time Jazz had thought she might somehow just walk away from the Stoker house.

"Take off the gag, Jeff," she said, "or we're no better than him."

"Of course," said the man, Jeff. "Sure. Desperate times, right? I'm Jeff Daws. My wife, Sherry."

He indicated the burned woman, then knelt closer and untied Jazz's gag, but not the other bonds.

Jazz spat to clear her mouth. "You're going to keep me tied up, though? Jesus, I must be so threatening to men."

"Shut up," said Daws.

"Am I your property now? Something you can lord over Stoker? Hey, look! I've got her panties now! She's all mine! Oog booga!

Daws slapped her across the face. Jazz fell back, crying and nodding to herself.

"Yeah," she mumbled. "'Cause *Stoker's* the asshole."

Daws looked ready to attack again but his wife stepped in. "Back off, Jeff." Then she turned to Jazz. "He's tracking you, you know. Stoker. We're not going to let you warn him or help him."

"I left him tied up..."

Daws spat on the ground. "Didn't tell us, did you? Didn't think about the people out here who are starving. Just trashed the place and thought about yourself. Because your kind never thinks about others! You're just like him!"

Jazz spasmed up almost to sitting. "I'M NOTHING LIKE

HIM! I'm a single girl trying to survive, and you *men* keep beating me and tying me up like I'm property! Because what? Everything you believed about civilized behavior was just a lie? The bomb falls and all bets are off? This is the *real* you?"

"Okay, now..."

"Is that what women are to you? Property? Is that what your wife is to you?"

"You got no right..."

"Clearly!" Jazz said. "And your talk before the bomb— yeah, I remember that—about people helping other people. Was that all bullshit?"

Jeff Daws shook his big, scarred head. "We're looking out for each other. You're not part of that."

"I'm a person. Look at me. Come close here and look at me."

Daws started to shuffle in, but Sherry stepped between him and Jazz, looking down at her with a cold face. "I see bait," she said.

"What?" Jazz said.

"Bait. Drawing Stoker to us. Nothing more."

She turned to stare down her husband until Jeff Daws stood up fully and skulked away. Sherry Daws grabbed a burning stick from the closest fire and came back to hold it up between her and Jazz as if she wanted to be able to see Jazz's face better, and have Jazz see hers.

"You know my husband's trying to do the right thing. Organizing us. Not taking advantage of anyone. 'Course, you're the first pretty one..."

The burning stick wavered closer to Jazz's face and Jazz spoke quickly to change that line of thought. "Why aren't you both dead?"

"We were behind our big fireplace. Saved us from the

initial blast, but not from burns or radiation." Sherry Daws unconsciously touched her burn scars.

"Your daughter doesn't look burned."

Sherry Daws nodded. "Annie was in the basement. We were all sleeping down there during renos on the main floor. So we holed up in the basement for a couple of days. Then we found a working truck and tried to drive out."

She fell silent, though she was clearly remembering. Jazz finally prodded her.

"What happened?"

There was a long pause as if Sherry Daws didn't want to relive it. Then her voice cracked and she began to speak, slowly, but with growing force, recalling so much detail that Jazz almost couldn't help but relive it with her.

Jeff Daws found the Ford pickup as he stumbled back from banging again on Stoker's basement door.

He would have missed it but for the sheer terror he'd felt at the sound of some other human pack calling out across the ruins from the direction of Carroll Street. And Daws without his backup. Daws all alone. Daws, wrapped head-to-toe up against the fires and radiation and trying to play hero by persuading his one-time neighbor to open up to him and share his provisions. Daws had planned to get enough fresh food or water back to Sherry and Annie and Christy and Jordan so that they could all try to make the hike towards the mountains.

But now he'd failed at that—Again! Dumbass!—and was out here all alone in the still crazy-hot rubble of the old neighborhood. And some other human pack that was ranging outside their home territory was going to find him and kill him or hold him hostage.

So Daws deliberately took a different route back towards Main, skittering around fires and climbing over broken walls and cars and who knew what all that reminded him powerfully of the way his daddy had used to preach about what things were like in Hell.

That's when he tripped and almost fell past a charcoaled telephone pole, rolled down a slope of rubble, and came to a stop with his nose pressed into the front fender of a truck grill with the half-melted "FORD" across it.

Everything from that logo on down was buried in dirt and rubble, which meant nothing to him for a couple beats, then Daws had worked his way around to the side and started digging furiously like a soft-handed badger. And uncovered actual tires! Unmelted rubber. As if the truck's loving owner had parked his baby in just such a way it would be sheltered from the main blast and the firestorm that had ripped through here after it.

Hallelujah!

And eighteen hours later, filthy and near collapse, his little pack had dug out the truck and even managed to sift through an impossible nightmare of the closest two houses to find crispy charred bodies and the right ignition key nestled inside some of the char.

An hour after that, with only Jeff Daws not semi-comatose in his seat—good thing, since he was driving—the truck of determined blast survivors from Redmond, Washington, turned onto NE Novelty Hill Road and slowed to a crawl as they approached the first signs of real civilization any of them had seen in days.

"Sherry, wake up!" Jeff barked. "Christy! Jordan!"

"What?" Jordan croaked from the passenger seat. "What the fuck?"

"A roadblock."

"Military?" Jordan said.

"Why?" Sherry added from the back, then shushed

Annie as the girl woke up, somehow sensed the distress in the truck's cab, and began to cry.

"What is it?" Christy moaned.

"What do we do?" Jordan said.

But before Jeff could do anything at all, the spotlights set up behind the parked army vehicles pinned them in their glare so that Jeff's foot came off the gas completely and the truck slowed to a halt.

Within seconds, four soldiers planted themselves out front with their rifles aimed through the windshield at Jeff. Four more swarmed the truck itself, shining their flashlights in through the windows.

The senior among them, who had made Jeff roll down his window and who had swung down his rifle long enough to take pictures of Jeff and the other occupants of the truck, now stepped back and made a hand signal over his head.

He shouted into the blazing spotlights, "Radiation burns! Too far gone!"

Then he turned back to Jeff and his pack. "I'm sorry, sir, but you have to turn around now. Go find some place to hold up. Wait for FEMA to come in. We don't have the resources out here to take care of you yet."

Jeff looked over at Jordan, back at Sherry and Annie, then back to the soldier. "How long's that going to be?"

"I can't say, sir," said the man who couldn't have been more than thirty but had raised his left hand to draw his comrades' attention to a possible threat. "Turn around. I'm going to repeat it one more time. Turn around *now*."

JEFF DAWS WAS SUDDENLY STANDING near Jazz's bent knees.

"We found out later," he said, "that they've got road blocks on every major road out. Small roads are unpassable."

"Impassable," Sherry corrected.

"We came back here. Found other survivors to join us. Now we scrounge for food and water. Dead in a week or two but we keep trying. For Annie."

"So it was you who pounded on our door at night."

"It's dangerous being out in the daytime," Sherry said. "Other survivor groups."

"Like Stoker said."

"Oh, yeah," Jeff Daws said. "He's a smart sonofabitch."

Jazz rolled over onto her other side to relieve the pain in her floor-side hip. "So what are you going to..."

"We take his supplies," Jeff Daws said. "Like we've taken yours. And we give him exactly what he's earned from all the survivors you see in this room tonight."

Jazz grimaced. "Revenge."

Jeff Daws shook his head. "Collective justice."

"And me?"

He chewed his lips. "Don't know yet."

"Let me help. He's my enemy too."

"You let him live."

She had. Why had she done that? Weakness? Squeamishness about killing? "That was a mistake, okay? I should have killed him and shared our supplies. I was scared."

A whistle call sounded from someone in the shadows and Jeff turned to see the signal. He nodded, then turned back and grabbed the gag that had been on Jazz before, stuffing it back into her mouth even as she started to protest.

Then, as the dark shapes beyond the fires scurried into the invisibility of their assigned posts, Jeff Daws pulled his wife close and spoke to her like Jazz had ceased to exist.

"Get Annie to the east corner and stay away from the windows.

"Are you sure..."

"Go!"

Jeff Daws pulled out a scorched handgun from his pocket and checked its chamber as Sherry hurried. Then he looked down at Jazz and said, "You try rolling out of the lit circle and we'll kick you back in. The first time. No guarantees you won't be shot if you try it twice."

Jazz nodded, but as Daws ran out of the circle into the darkness, she began frantically looking around for something to cut her bonds with.

CHAPTER 40

STOKER SLOWLY CIRCLED the store some thirty yards out.

The lights within said people. The fact they didn't seem to be trying to hide it told him it was probably a trap. Maybe for other unsuspecting survivors, but Stoker had enough ego to believe it was for him. The faces he'd seen moving in the shadows had probably reported on him to whomever was in charge now. Because even when civilization broke down into chaos, someone always took charge. Most people were sheep. It wasn't that hard.

It also stood to reason that they had Jasmine. If they'd spotted him, they'd have spotted her because she'd been traveling the same path, just a little ways ahead.

And they would have just taken her. Less of a threat.

All of which meant that he couldn't just pass by this little stronghold. No. It held the woman he loved. Probably supplies, too, which he could use to sustain him and Jasmine when they continued on out of the fallout zone.

He zigged his way in closer, using the wall of a building to the left of the store for cover. When he stopped at the gap between the buildings, he could see across what used to be an alleyway in through a shattered window. There was a dark shape bunched in the lower corner of it. Probably someone with a gun.

He picked his way towards the back of the destroyed building he was in to come at the stronghold from the rear. And this time he was able to slip across the gap to a rear corner window—all the glass gone here, too—and peer in.

He saw Jasmine immediately. On the floor in a ring of small fires. She was bound like an animal. Sickening. Though he supposed he could see the logic behind it. She couldn't jump up and escape with him even if he distracted everyone else in the building.

And that was the second problem, of course. Identifying how many people there were in there and where they hid.

Stoker closed his eyes to let them reacquire their night vision, then opened and deliberately avoided looking at the fires or bright area around Jazz. He was able to pick three people at different windows, plus what looked like a woman and a restless child hiding against the back east wall. But there were piles of junk throughout the room. Too many places for shooters to hide.

Stoker slid away from the window and thought hard. If there were more than three or four with guns, there was no way he'd get to Jasmine without getting shot. He'd have to take most of them out first. Using nothing but a single pistol and a lot of luck.

Should he just leave then? Abandon Jasmine?

But he loved her. He was pretty sure of that.

In any case he had earned her. He'd saved her life. Cared for her. Won her affection, however briefly. He knew he could make her love him again.

"Fuck it," he whispered.

He bent and picked up a piece of rubble, stepped out

from the building, and chucked it at the next window along the wall towards the street side of the building. It hit and rattled into the building.

A rustle from inside told Stoker the face he'd seen in the furthest street-side window was hustling back to check it out. Stoker ducked his head back into the furthest-back window he'd looked in earlier, tracked the running shape with his gun, and fired two quick shots to take him down.

As the body dropped, the firelight caught his face. A teenage boy.

And across the middle of the floor ran a second shape, a teen girl, firing in Stoker's direction. Hitting the wall well to his left.

Stoker raised his gun, steadied his arm, and fired two more quick shots. *Blam. Blam.* The girl went down.

From somewhere an older female voice cried, "Nooo!" and a horribly burned woman stepped out from behind a pile of shopping carts and warped metal bookcase. She raised a shotgun and started firing at Stoker's window.

*BOOM! BOOM!*

Stoker jerked back outside, then jumped back up and shot back, taking down the woman and three more shapes that had been running towards him. *Blam. Blam. Blam. Blam. Blam. Blam.*

"I'm going to save you, Jazz!" he called in.

Then he ducked down and ran for the back of the building, changing out the nearly empty clip for his one full one as he went.

CHAPTER 41

Against the wall nearest Jazz, Jeff Daws had his pistol up.

He was on the other side of the fires from Jazz but she swore she could hear his breathing and see his nostrils flare as he followed the fight and how badly it was going.

Jazz herself had twitched back and forth where she lay on the floor, trying to follow the action, but most of her attention had been focused on the jagged piece of concrete she held between her fingers and tried to use as a crude saw on the ropes that bound her. They were thicker than plastic zip ties, but they also gave more as she twisted about. Whether Stoker killed everyone in here or Daws' people managed to take him down, Jazz wasn't going to just lie here and wait to find out. No way.

The entire room had gone still for the moment. Besides the constant sound of fires burning and wind blowing outside, silence reigned.

Jazz looked back towards Daws and saw him wave a dark-skinned man towards the backside of the store.

Towards the window nearest where Sherry Daws huddled with Annie.

The dark man nodded and loped silently in that direction, carrying a sawed-off shotgun.

Stillness again. But there was groaning from the wounded on the floor and a steady *drip, drip, drip* of blood from the dead.

Suddenly a portion of the fire-eaten roof collapsed almost directly over the head of Sherry and Annie Daws.

They shrieked as the timbers and rubble and crap fell, then shrieked again when they realized Stoker had dropped down with it. He jumped to his feet now, spun, and shot the dark-skinned man running from the nearby window. The big man staggered backwards, clutched the side of his head, and went down. Then Stoker grabbed Annie and kicked Sherry so hard in her legs that the mother stumbled and fell and Stoker knelt on top of her.

One of Stoker's arms circled Annie's neck. The other pressed the muzzle of his pistol into the side of Sherry's head.

"Okay, Jeff!" he called out. "Game's over! Got your little girl and wifey here! Step into the light or I'm gonna do what a nuclear bomb couldn't!"

Jeff Daws was suddenly directly behind Jazz, holding her torso up in front of him like a human shield.

"And maybe I'll kill off your little honey!" he yelled back at Stoker. "Hunh? Blow her brains out right here!"

"I don't know if she's even alive!" Stoker said. "Take off her gag! Have her say something!"

Jeff fumbled with the gag. Then he gave up and pulled out the hunting knife he'd stolen from Jazz. He used it to saw through the gag. As it came loose, Jazz spat it from her mouth.

"Talk to me, Jasmine!" Stoker called.

"I'm...I'm good," Jazz said. "The baby..."

"Still think you were better heading out alone?"

"Not so much."

"But I'm here now. It's all going to work out."

Jeff covered Jazz's mouth with a hand and she shook her head but couldn't throw it off.

"We do a swap," Jess said. "Her for my wife and daughter."

"Bring her closer," Stoker said.

"You want me to untie her?"

"Uh...sure," Stoker said. "I mean, please do."

So Jeff reached down for the ropes with his knife and Jazz almost screamed in frustration. She'd almost freed her*self*, assholes. Just a few more minutes...

Jeff paused a minute as he saw the frayed condition of the ropes. Then he cut all the ropes so that Jazz's ankles and wrists again sprung free.

Before she could even massage them or get them moving again, though, Jeff grabbed one of her freed hands, put the hunting knife into it, and whispered in her ear, "Prove to me you're a person."

He guided her hand to slip the knife down the back waistband of her jeans, then he hauled her up to her feet.

Jazz unkinked with grunts of pain, not knowing now what to think of Daws, what he expected her to do. Why shouldn't she just stab him right now and go diving out a window?

*Prove to me you're a person.*

Versus what? Chattel? Something to be bargained back and forth by men? The spoils of war? A manipulable, emotional, weak thing who could be bullied, directed, and used as a pawn?

"Bring her forward," Stoker said.

So Jeff Daws started to do so. Both he and Jazz jumped as Annie's cat ran between them so that Jazz almost stepped on it.

"Sorry!" Jazz said. "Sorry, sorry, sorry."

"Keep coming!" Stoker ordered. "It can't bring you worse luck than you've already had."

When they were a couple yards apart, Jeff Daws pulled Jazz to a stop.

"Let my daughter go," he said. "You'll still have my wife. Show you can bargain in good faith."

"Is that lawyer talk?" Stoker said. "Or were you member of a union, Jeff? Or a union organizer? Right! I remember. Bet all these people in here were glad they followed you."

But he let go of Annie anyway and the little girl ran to stand behind her daddy.

"Now this next bit is trickier, isn't it?" said Jeff. "I have your woman, young as she is..."

"And pregnant," Stoker said. "But you knew that, didn't you. Tying up a pregnant woman."

"Okay. Okay," said Jeff. "So let's keep it simple. I count to three, and on three we each release our respective hostages and just...go our own ways."

Stoker nodded. "Remarkably sensible for a union guy."

"One. Two. Three."

Jeff Daws released Jazz. Stoker released Sherry. Stoker and Jeff both raised their pistols to shoot but Stoker was quicker. *Blam!* Jeff Daws' brains splattered backwards over his daughter's head and he crumpled down as she shrieked.

Sherry Daws ran to her, clutching her to her breast and turning her back towards Stoker.

Stoker snorted. "Like I would shoot an unarmed mother

in her back? Jazz, pick up Jeff's gun, please, and give it to me."

Jazz did, forcing herself not to watch Sherry as she held Annie a little to one side and knelt beside her husband's corpse. She did note how closely Stoker watched, his gun pointed her way, as Jazz scooped up Daws' dropped pistol.

Jazz walked to him with the gun, her steps shaky, her entire being devastated, almost in shock. It wasn't much of an acting stretch.

"They were going to kill me," she said as she handed him Jeff's pistol.

Stoker stuck the pistol into one of the pockets on the front of his flak jacket, then said, "Kiss me, Jasmine. All is forgiven."

She leaned in to do so briefly and stayed up close, breathing into his cheek.

"You know what you've taught me with all of this?" she said.

"What, my dear?"

"That power isn't so much about the hand life has dealt me. It's about being smart, being one hundred percent clear on who I am, and, being able to lie so well to assholes who deserve it that they actually want to protect me."

"What?"

He started to pull back from her, but Jazz's hand already had the knife from her rear waistband. The knife Jeff Daws had given her. After stealing it from her. After she'd stolen it from Stoker. A knife that wanted to go home.

Jazz drove it with all her might up under Stoker's flak jacket and it entered his gut with a wet, sucking sound.

She lost her grip on it as Stoker half-twisted and jerked backwards.

CHAPTER 42

"You...you can't," Stoker said.

He was trying to raise the pistol he still held in his right hand. The one from the lockbox that he'd refused her when she left the shelter. She grabbed it from him now. He stumbled backwards and sat. Then fell over on his side. Jazz stepped to him and carefully plucked Daws' gun from Stoker's flak jacket pocket.

She aimed the lockbox gun into his face, her hand shaking.

"I'm not pregnant. Not from Aaron. And if you knocked me up..."

Behind her, the dark-skinned defender Stoker had shot earlier, groaned back up to his feet. "Shoot him," he said now with a thick accent that might have been Jamaican.

"I'd like to," Jazz said. "Really. He's a raping, murdering asshole. But enough people have died."

Stoker watched her from where he lay on his side. He'd managed to pull the knife from his belly and now had both hands clutched over the wound. Clearly couldn't get up.

Couldn't move. His face was white and sweaty. But he wasn't dead yet.

The dark-skinned man turned to Sherry, who was still collapsed over her husband. "Sherry," he said. "Others may be alive."

In her peripheral vision, Jazz saw Sherry Daws visibly pull herself together and tug Annie close to her. She whispered in Annie's ear. A second later, the young girl took off running into the darkness by the windows. Jazz half-saw her stop at a lumpen shape on the ground, shake it, wait, shake it again, then run on to another.

After a moment, Annie called out, "Christy's 'live!" And another moment after that, "Jordan's 'live!"

When Jazz glanced over, she saw Annie helping a young man she assumed was Jordan to his feet. As he got closer, Jazz realized he was only a teenager, seventeen at most, baby face covered with burns, tall skinny body and gangly arms not swinging a shotgun up and pointing it angrily at Jazz and Stoker, shouting, "Why aren't they dead?"

Behind him and Annie, an even younger teen, a girl, presumably Christy, was also staggering over to join them, one hand trying to stanch the blood oozing from her side.

The dark-skinned defender walked to Jordan and pushed down the barrel of his shotgun. Then he turned to Jazz. "In this world now, girl," he said, "the rules is different. This man gotta die. You want to die too?"

Jazz looked at Sherry Daws. "Sherry?"

Sherry pulled Annie close to her again and turned away.

"Okay," Jazz said. "I've got a deal for you. I give him to you for fifteen minutes to *punish*, not kill..."

"*What?*" Stoker croaked behind her.

The maybe-Jamaican shook his head. "Man gotta die, girl. Last chance."

"And in exchange for letting him live," Jazz said directly to Sherry, "and letting us both walk out of here alive, I'll take Annie with us through the barricade. Because she's healthy, right? She goes with me and Professor Stoker, they'll let us all through."

Jordan was shaking his head furiously and trying to wrestle the barrel of his shotgun away from the Jamaican. "Let me fucking shoot them!"

Sherry whipped her face back towards him. "NO!" She left Annie and ran to Jordan, tearing the shotgun from the two men holding it and shoving Jordan backwards. Then Sherry turned and, hands shaking, pointed the shotgun at Jazz.

"How do I know it's not a trick?" she said. Her voice quavered and her fingers clenched around the forestock and trigger guard so hard her knuckles were white. "How do we know you won't just dump her halfway there?"

"What other chance does she have?" Jazz said.

Sherry fired the shotgun so close over Jazz's head that for a second, Jazz thought she was hit. She dropped to her hands and knees and saw blood drip down. Felt her bloody scalp and realized bits of shot must have grazed her.

"I'm not giving my child over to be abused!" Sherry cried.

"Mad bitch," Stoker muttered.

Sherry stepped in closer and aimed the shotgun squarely into Stoker's face, driving Jazz back up to her feet, knocking the gun to one side.

"No!" she said. "Sherry, no. Look, when I lost my dad to cancer, my mom to a car accident, I...gave up. But then this guy's twisted assholery actually made me want to live again.

And I guess I want to make sure it counts. So let me help your daughter, Annie. Let me give her a chance to live. With me."

Sherry lowered her shotgun and hid her face, her chest heaving. The Jamaican was less impressed.

"We get him for fifteen minutes," he said. "Say no and we kill you both now."

Stoker cleared his throat. "Look, is this really necessary? I'll be a much better help with Annie if—"

"Shut up!" Sherry snapped, jerking up her shotgun again.

Jazz swallowed and placed her two pistols on the ground. She backed away from them and Stoker.

The Jamaican limped in and grabbed the guns. Then he hoisted the groaning Stoker up and carried him towards the door. Jordan and Christy followed.

Sherry whispered something to Annie, then followed the others out the door.

Annie ran to Jazz. The girl's cat joined them.

"His name's Tiger," Annie said. "He likes you."

"Okay," Jazz said.

It was just her and the girl, a flickering ring of sputtering fires, and corpses, including that of Annie's father. How could this little girl not be traumatized? Or had she really seen so much over the last week that she was beyond that. The fact she was petting her cat and not huddled up in a little ball scared the hell out of Jazz.

"C'mere, Annie," she said and pulled the little girl close, wrapping her in tight and covering her ears just as Jazz heard whumps and hissing sounds. And Stoker's screams.

They went on and on.

CHAPTER 43

WHEN THEY WERE DONE with Stoker, Christy fetched Jazz and Annie outside with the others. The ring of them stood in the dark like bloody, exhausted statues, their faces lit by the flickering of a nearby fire.

On the road, a few feet away, its motor running, was a half-burned minivan, its engine running.

"He's in the back," Sherry told Jazz. "He'll live."

"How do you know that?" Jazz said.

"I'm a nurse. Was a nurse. I think your knife somehow missed everything important or he'd be dead by now. I bound him up."

"Um…"

"If you make it out…"

"I'll protect her. I'll love her."

Jazz looked down at Annie as she said it. The girl had her cat in her arms and watched the exchange with wide eyes that seemed to understand more than they possibly could.

"Tiger, too," she said.

"Of course," Jazz said.

She opened the driver's door of the van and Annie clambered in and across to the passenger's seat. There she settled herself and struggled but managed to clip in the seatbelt like she'd done this before. No biggie.

Jazz climbed in, closed the door, and settled too. She tried to ignore the smell of blood and burnt flesh from the back as she put the van in gear and began to drive.

CHAPTER 44

THE SPEED LIMIT was irrelevant because the way was so littered with debris that Jazz rarely took the minivan over fifteen miles per hour. She wove it back and forth and had to backtrack twice to find alternate routes, leaning hard on her innate sense of direction because the smoky night sky obscured any distant sight of the Cascade mountains.

Even worse, the further she drove from downtown Seattle, the fewer fires there were, which made it hard to see the road. So they jolted in and out of potholes, over rubble. Jazz found herself muttering regular prayers the tires would hold up.

"You know what this looks like?" she said to Annie, who was still wide awake. Shock, Jazz thought. Or permanent PTSD. "This looks like my dreams of driving. Totally lost. Maybe going in the right direction, but absolutely no way to know."

A moan sounded from the area behind the rear seats.

"Real helpful, Professor!" Jazz called back. "Thanks so much for those words of—"

She stopped as a blinding set of lights switched on

directly ahead. Jazz slammed on the brakes. The minivan skidded to a halt.

The sight of soldiers running out around the minivan and shining their flashlights in through the windows probably would have terrified Jazz if she hadn't already heard Sherry's story of it happening to them. So she just put a hand on Annie to reassure her and rolled down her own window.

After some whispering between the soldiers, the one in charge came to her window.

"Where are you from?" he said.

"Further in. We were in a concrete basement when the bomb hit. We had earthquake supplies. We waited for the fires to die down, then drove out here. We're all pretty healthy, but we could sure use a bath."

"The guy in the back..."

"An asshole. But it was actually his basement we were in. His supplies. Unfortunately, he ticked off some people we met on the way out. They exacted a toll." Off his expression, she hurried to say, "It's not radiation burns you see there. Just regular burns...and stuff."

"Are you lying to me right now?"

The soldier shone the flashlight directly into Jazz's face. She blinked but didn't look away.

"No, sir," she said. "That may not be the whole story. But it's pretty close."

The soldier held the light on her a beat longer, then withdrew and turned towards the spotlights. He raised his hand and chopped it back and forth.

"They're healthy!" he shouted. "Let 'em out!"

"PULL DOWN MY SHEET," Stoker ordered the interviewer.

The young woman pursed her lips. "I don't think…"

"You've read the report," Stoker said. "Don't you want to see what they did to me? You needn't worry about my modesty. I'm wearing diapers."

The young woman clicked off her recording device and reversed it to just before his request. Then she stepped to the room's door and locked it. When she returned, she took the top edges of his bedsheet between her fingers and slowly pulled it down…

…to reveal burned, scraped-up shoulders, chest, and stomach, the last also home to a nasty-looking set of stitches where he'd been knifed.

And he wore adult hospital diapers, as he'd said.

But what made the interviewers gorge rise in her mouth was the fact Stoker was a quadruple amputee. Yes, she'd read the report. How his limbs had been burned, then hacked off and cauterized with yet more fire. Then bound, his stomach crudely stitched and taped. The punishment for those he'd killed in his "rescue" of Jasmine Kazmi. But actually seeing it...

As the interviewer hurried to raise the sheet up again, Stoker shook his head violently.

"Leave it! It's too damn hot in this room anyway."

"All right," she said. She swallowed her bile and re-took her seat. She turned the recorder back on. "So is that the end of your story?"

"It is," Stoker said. "China and Russia fuck America. I fuck Jasmine. She and her blast buddies fuck me. You and your provisional government fuck her blast buddies. Fear and suspicion win. The social order prevails. And all the rats are running through a maze they don't even know they're in."

His voice had risen as he spoke and his face flushed red. But the young woman interviewing him didn't buy it. It was a performance. Everything with this man was a performance.

"You'll pardon me if I don't accept the analysis of an admitted rapist," she said.

"But it's all true. You'd know if you could watch my fingers. No tapping at all. Trust me."

"Ha. Ha."

A knock on the door kept him from pushing it further. The interviewer rose, unlocked the door and opened it. Jasmine Kazmi entered. The interviewer knew Kazmi by her picture in the file, but it had been one of the other privates in the Washington militia who'd done the intake interview with her.

Yet after the story she'd just heard, the interviewer hardly expected the cleaned up, fresh, happy looking person who stood before her now.

"May I?" Kazmi asked her and gestured at the uncovered Stoker where he lay on his bed.

The interviewer studied her closely for a moment longer, thinking: *My age. My general height. Darker skin and hair, but...not so different from me.*

The interviewer nodded. "I'm done with him. He's all yours." And she left the room, closing the door behind her.

CHAPTER 46

JAZZ WATCHED the young woman go. Blonde hair chopped short for duty, but pretty, smart, and not entirely sure of herself. Exactly Stoker's type.

Jazz shook her head in amused disgust and turned back to Stoker. She walked to the chair the interviewer had been seated in and pulled it closer to Stoker's bed. Finding the hospital bed controls, she powered the top half of his bed back down so Stoker lay flat on his back.

"Jesus, thank you," he said. "Nobody considers that half-sitting up for hours on end when you don't have legs or arms to steady yourself is an act of heroic endurance."

"I'm sure it is."

"And the questions! Very few had to do with me, by the way. Everything's about you. 'How did Jasmine survive? How did she rescue you and little Annie?'"

"You've been telling stories about me?"

He grinned at her. "The whole adventure."

"What you knew of it."

"Of course. I guessed at the things I wasn't sure of."

Jazz nodded. "I wanted to thank you, Professor. For

helping me get rid of all the mental zip ties I let hold me down. I'm going to write my own story now."

She leaned in and kissed him lightly on the forehead. When she pulled back, his eyes glistened. So she lingered just a moment more.

"Call me in a few days," he said. "Just to talk. Reminisce. Discuss how the war's going."

And the real testament to how much she had moved on was that she felt no need to strangle him at that moment. Nor hit him. Nor rage at him. By some divine insight, Sherry Daws and the other doomed survivors had found the best possible punishment for someone so tied to his physical obsessions as Stoker was. The only thing better might have been to remove his tongue.

Maybe if Jazz ever saw him again...

She smiled at him and, without a word, walked out of the room.

She found Annie in the hallway where she'd left her, sitting on the floor with her amazingly forbearing cat held tightly in her lap. The little girl was going through a time of clinging, crying, night terrors, and anger, and Jazz couldn't have been happier. Maybe over the years she and Annie could do therapy together until all the evil times they been through and the things they had lost were just done and gone. Not forgotten, but stripped of their power to hurt.

From back in the interview room, Stoker called after her, "I'm your history! The only one who will ever know what you went through! You need me!"

Jazz knelt in front of Annie. "Oh, I don't think we do, do we, Annie?"

"Uh-unh," Annie said.

Jazz scooped up her and her cat and walked with them out of the building and into the sunlight.

Terry Hayman lives with his family in the Pacific Northwest, where he writes screenplays, novels, and short fiction. You can find more about him and his work at www.terryhayman.com.

## AN OPPORTUNITY

Hi,

I hope you enjoyed the read. If you'd like to find out about more of my work and what I have in the pipeline, go to www.terryhayman.com and subscribe to my mailing list.

You'll also get access to goodies like fiction exclusive to members of my mailing list, previews of new cover designs, maybe the disclosure of some of my pen names, and the chance to share your thoughts and feedback on any number of creative things I'm doing.

As members of my list, you get heard because I value your voice and readership.

Go to www.terryhayman.com and subscribe and you'll get a FREE PDF of THE FIRST STORY I EVER SOLD!

*Chasing the Minotaur*

*Jessica Falls*

*Raised by a Vampire*

**Collections**

*Being Human*

*Off World*

*Dark Paths*

*Life Knots*

*Used by Magic*

*Shorties*

*Vamp*